"Not going to talk?"

She swiveled her head back around, trying to ignore the throbbing headache that was building from the point of injury. "I can't."

Bowen's expression darkened. "You can't."

Lainey swallowed a sudden need to cry. To expel emotion bottled within her from the fear of the afternoon's events. "I can't," she repeated.

Don't expose yourself. That had been rule number one, the marshal assigned to her case had said. *Never give your real name. Don't try to contact your family or friends. As far as you're concerned, the life you lived doesn't exist anymore.*

Granted, there were some allowances, Lainey had discovered. For one, the FBI did offer to help her make contact with her parents once a year, if she needed. But she hadn't. The fear of Uncle Chris was real and Lainey had been worried he could issue retribution even from behind bars. Apparently, she'd been right.

"WITSEC?"

Bowen's intuition stunned Lainey. She stared at him. Words choked her throat. Everything in her wanted to tell him—well, tell him everything. But did she dare?

Jaime Jo Wright is an ECPA bestselling author and multi-award winner—including the Christy and Daphne du Maurier Awards. She is coffee-fueled and a cat-fancier extraordinaire and resides in Wisconsin's rural woodlands. Her literary vocation involves penning chilling tales, with a strong preference to the master of dark, Edgar Allan Poe. Visit her at jaimewrightbooks.com and listen to her podcast, *MadLit Musings*, on YouTube or your favorite podcast player.

Books by Jaime Jo Wright

Love Inspired Suspense

Buried Wilderness Secrets
Attempted Mountain Murder

Visit the Author Profile page at LoveInspired.com.

ATTEMPTED MOUNTAIN MURDER

JAIME JO WRIGHT

LOVE INSPIRED® SUSPENSE
INSPIRATIONAL ROMANCE

Recycling programs for this product may not exist in your area.

ISBN-13: 978-1-335-95784-9

Attempted Mountain Murder

Copyright © 2026 by Jaime Sundsmo

Love Inspired
22 Adelaide St. West, 41st Floor
Toronto, Ontario M5H 4E3, Canada
www.LoveInspired.com

HarperCollins Publishers
Macken House, 39/40 Mayor Street Upper,
Dublin 1, D01 C9W8, Ireland
www.HarperCollins.com

Printed in Lithuania

1 2 3 4 5 6 7 8 9 10 LIT 28 27 26 25

The Lord shall preserve thee from all evil:
he shall preserve thy soul. The Lord shall preserve
thy going out and thy coming in from this time forth,
and even for evermore.
—*Psalm* 121:7–8

To the Masterminds.
Kimberley Woodhouse, Jayna Breigh,
Tracie Peterson, Jocelyn Green, Amanda Dykes,
Darcie Gudger and Becca Whitham.
You all are my cheerleaders.
Minus pom-poms and insert coffee/tea mugs.

ONE

Her apartment was ransacked. Couch pillows had been sliced open, their stuffing shed on the floor. Books were tossed from the bookshelf by the front door, a painting of a wildflower garden hung at a cockeyed angle on the white wall, and the drawers of the entertainment stand were open. Lainey Jo Beckett stared at it all. The shock of it stunned her. She had known fear before, but she hadn't missed it. Now it returned with a vengeance.

It wasn't just that her place had been tossed—it was the fact that she had been found. She started to cross the room, eyeing the chaos in disbelief. Without warning, something shattered the glass of her living room window and sliced a painful graze across her temple. Lainey Jo threw herself onto the living room floor, her tongue stinging as her teeth bit into it on impact. Her palms burned against the cream carpet beneath her. A bullet lodged into the opposite wall, but Lainey Jo ignored it—she tried to ignore the searing pain on the side of her head too, as she crawled back across the floor toward the door.

"Oh God, please help me." Lainey Jo didn't bother to whisper her prayer. There was no one inside her apartment to fear, only outside. Had the sniper been the one to tear apart her home? Or had there been another person too? Maybe her assumption that she was alone wasn't true!

She made her way over the mess on the floor, her knees and palms pressing into books that lay every which way. Lainey Jo paid no attention to her head wound and how it stained the open pages of *Treasure Island*. Her beloved classics meant nothing to her. They weren't her originals. Nothing in this apartment was original, or even really hers. She had merely pretended for the last few years. Somehow, it had all caught up with her.

A lamp was broken, and now her legs crunched over its glass along with the shards from the window. She could feel them stabbing through her jeans, but she didn't dare stand. Someone had shot at her through her window! All she could do now was try to escape alive.

She managed to push herself to her feet as she reached the door. She was just out of sight of her window now, but who might be standing on the other side of the door? Or— Lainey Jo gave the small apartment a quick sweep of her attention—who might leap out from the closet or the bathroom at any moment? She palmed the doorknob to the front door. If she flung it open and sprinted, could she escape anyone who may be on their way to finish her?

Uncle Chris had masterminded this. Lainey Jo knew it— she just didn't know how. He was behind bars, and she'd helped put him there before entering the Witness Protection Program. But he was powerful, and he held grudges, and somehow, he had found her.

Without waiting another second, Lainey Jo opened the door, a hitch in her breath as she half expected someone to be on the other side, ready to put a bullet through her. But the hallway to the apartment was empty, aside from the door opposite her opening a crack. The concerned and inquisitive eyes of her video gamer neighbor stared out at her.

"You okay?" he inquired.

She waved him off, irritated. "Get back inside."

"I heard a gun—"

"Get back inside!" Lainey Jo stumbled, disoriented from her head wound.

Her neighbor opened his door wider, his eyes growing larger at the sight of blood running down the side of her face. "I'll call 911!"

"No!" she half shouted, shuffling away from him as she tripped down the hallway toward the stairwell exit. The police wouldn't be of any help. She needed to call Marshal Halloway. He was the one assigned to her case. He would understand the nuances. But first, she needed to get to safety, and that wasn't here.

The stairwell door slammed behind her and cut off whatever her neighbor was shouting after her. Lainey Jo catapulted down the stairs, gripping onto the handrail to stay upright. If it *had* been a trained sniper who'd taken the shot at her, then it was only by God's grace that she was even alive. God's grace hadn't seemed to play well with her since bringing down Uncle Chris and his human trafficking ring, but then, one could argue that she was paying for the sins of her family. Somehow, they had lived their luxurious lifestyle, she'd gone to private schools, vacationed in the Mediterranean, all while Uncle Chris ruined lives right under their noses.

Dear Uncle Chris, whom Lainey Jo had grown up thinking hung the moon and stars. Uncle Chris, who, her father Scott proudly boasted, was the family's business savant, and Uncle Chris, who always showered her with gifts and affection.

She had taken him down. She had testified at his trial. She had avoided his eyes. That narrowed-eyed, dark glare that oozed betrayal at her. Uncle Chris loved hard—or so he'd always claimed—and now he hated equally so.

Lainey Jo burst from the door at the back of the apartment building, sucking in a desperate gasp of fresh air. She hoped since she'd exited the back that she was well out of range and scope of her would-be killer. But the fact that her car was parked at the front of the building and in the line of sight of the shooter was a definite problem. She was on foot in the Wyoming town of Sheridan, and it would be just as easy to be found as it would be hard to flee.

She swept the area around her. Lainey Jo was in the apartment complex's back parking lot. Across the street was a small grocery store. The kind that sold only organic fruits and vegetables, grass-fed beef and gluten-free bread. She'd never shopped there. She couldn't. Not on the hourly wage of a retail store manager. Her occupational qualifications on entering WITSEC had been abysmal, and her prior experience in retail shopping therapy had overqualified her.

But now, Lainey Jo hurried across the parking lot, scanning left and right, nervous that someone was going to jump out. A white van, perhaps—the kind without windows—would come squealing around the corner, doors open, a man jumping out to tug a pillowcase over her head and drag her into the vehicle. They'd take her somewhere. Kill her. Dump her body. Uncle Chris would eat his supper behind bars, a self-satisfied smile on his face.

A car drove past, and then a truck. Lainey Jo hesitated at the street, holding her hand over the wound on her head. It was throbbing now. A pulsating throb that made shutters begin to close on her eyes. She couldn't lose consciousness. Not here. Not on the side of a street.

The door of the apartment complex shut with a resounding thud. Lainey Jo twisted to dart a gaze over her shoulder. A man exited, the black cargo jacket over dark jeans and black combat boots an almost sure identification that he was the one out to kill her. There *had* been another person inside her apartment—or at least the complex! There was no way a sniper would have caught up to her this fast.

Lainey Jo surged into the street, holding her hand out, palm forward as if the motion alone would stop the car that careened toward her. Brakes squealed. She sprinted forward, barely evading a bruising collision with the vehicle. The driver shouted at her, but Lainey Jo ignored them. She shot another frantic glance over her shoulder. The man had disappeared.

This was bad. Very bad.

Lainey Jo noticed a man who'd come from the grocery store opening the driver's side door of his truck. An old, beat-up gray pickup with rusty fenders and a cracked windshield. He twisted in the driver's seat, setting a paper bag filled with groceries in the back seat.

A guy carrying organic groceries? Yes. Please. Far safer than whoever was pressing in behind her. Lainey Jo expected a bullet to slam into her back at any moment. But the cars, the few people in view—maybe the lack of anonymity is what stopped the bullet from coming.

Lainey Jo focused on the truck.

She had no other escape plan.

A rusty truck and a guy who had no idea what was about to happen.

Bowen half chucked the paper bag of groceries onto the back seat. Eighty-six bucks for a head of lettuce, a package of beef steaks, a box of chickpea macaroni and a few other odds and ends? He crumpled the receipt in his hand. He'd file-13 that in Gramma Lou's kitchen garbage when he got home.

"All right, Zeke, let's go." Bowen gave the truck's dash a fond tap with his hand. The truck had served him well the past year and a half since his time pulling active duty as a navy SEAL had ended. If it wasn't for Gramma Lou, he'd have disappeared into the mountains that hovered in the distance. But there were some things that even the worst of circumstances couldn't beat out of a SEAL, and one of them was their loyalty.

He turned the key in the ignition. Zeke roared to life, kudos to a stellar engine. Bowen reached for the shifter to shift into Reverse when the passenger side door flung open.

"What in the—"

A woman launched into the seat, slamming the door behind her. Blood ran down the right side of her face. Her honey-brown hair was disheveled and hung tangled over her shoulders. Bowen's quick sweep of her person told him she had abrasions on her legs, on her hands, and the head wound was eerily reminiscent of ones he'd seen on deployment.

"Go, go, go!" she shouted, pounding the dash, twisting around in her seat, terrified.

"What's going on?" Bowen didn't react to her command.

"Please." Desperation made the woman's voice quiver now. "Please get me out of here." She slid down into the seat as if she were trying to get out of view.

"I gotta bad feeling about this," Bowen muttered, putting Zeke into Reverse and backing out from his parking spot. He scanned the area as he did so. Nothing raised any alarms in his gut aside from the woman bleeding beside him.

Pulling out of the parking lot, Bowen shot her a sideways glance. "Tell me what's going on."

It was a directive. He expected her to respond.

She did. "I—I got home and someone shot at me through my window."

"Ground level?" Bowen turned right, heading toward the main drag through town. He'd take her to the ER. They could call the cops from there.

"N-no," she stuttered, drawing in a shuddering breath. "My apartment is on the third floor."

Third floor? Bowen frowned. That was no drive-by shooting. A renegade bullet? Some idiot cleaning his gun from across the street, and the gun misfired? The trajectory was possible, depending on where it came from.

"My apartment was ransacked." She blew out the air she'd just drawn in. "Everything is a mess."

"Any valuables taken?" Bowen flicked his turn signal on as he pulled up at a stop sign. He checked his six in the rearview mirror. He was confident the woman in the mini-van wrenching a sippy cup from her toddler in the back seat was not a threat.

"I don't know." His uninvited companion whimpered. "I don't know!"

"Okay. Take it easy. Let's get you to the ER and—"

"No!" Her hand shot out and grabbed at his arm.

Bowen glanced at her. Huge brown eyes filled with fear gutted him. "The police then." He could change coordinates and head there.

"No!" Her plea was watery this time. Desperate. Unsure.

"Ma'am, you need medical help."

"Just—do you have a phone? I just need to make a call."

He tugged his phone from his jeans pocket and handed it to her. Bowen still aimed his car for the ER. The woman was probably half out of her mind with that head wound.

Bowen noticed her fingers quivering as she tried to dial

a number. He directed his attention back to the road but furrowed his brows. That wasn't a local area code she'd punched in. The injured woman held the phone to her ear. After a few seconds, she whimpered and ended the call.

"I don't know what to do. I don't know what to do!" She bent at the waist, holding her head between her hands.

"Let's get you some help." Bowen's attempt to offer comfort and help was aborted as quickly as it was deployed.

"I said, no hospital. No police." This time, there was steel in her voice. She glared at him.

"Well, Calamity Jane, what do you want me to do with you then?" Bowen couldn't hide the ire in his tone. She'd all but stripped any options from him besides driving her around in Zeke until she told him where to drop her off.

He didn't expect her hand to latch onto his knee. There was nothing to it but warmth, fear and some innate instinct a woman had to grab hold of what she perceived to be strength and security.

"Someone is trying to kill me," she pleaded. "Just get me far away from here. Please."

Bowen bit back a growl of irritation. No hospital, no police? Who was this woman? Bowen wished he could just drop her off somewhere of her choosing and leave her. But that didn't sit well with him. It wasn't in his DNA to do that.

Fine. He could give her medical care at Gramma Lou's and assess the situation. Decision made, Bowen turned his car in the direction of the mountains. Besides, the woman would be better off under Gramma Lou's care anyway. People had a habit of dying when he was around.

"What did you bring home?" The gray-haired woman wiped her hands on a dish towel as she stepped out onto the porch of a small cabin nestled in the woods. She had a low ponytail, wore jeans and a rose-colored flannel shirt. Lainey Jo guessed she was probably in her early seventies. But she had pep, Lainey Jo had to give her that. There was nothing *old* about this woman.

The man she'd half accosted, half hijacked, had already opened her door and was helping her out. She pressed a sweatshirt her rescuer had given her to her head wound, but Lainey Jo still battled lightheadedness. The cabin was in a secluded area, surrounded by trees, with a rich, earthy smell in the air along with a distinct scent of woodsmoke emanating from the cabin's chimney. A front porch was inviting, with a porch swing and a few pots of red geraniums that would hang on to their blossoms until the freeze finally came.

Lainey Jo shivered. It was early fall, but there was a chill in the air. Not to mention her whole body was beginning to shake for entirely different reasons. She bit back a sob as her knees buckled.

"Whoa there." The man hefted her up with an arm around her waist, holding her steady. Lainey Jo didn't miss the fact that he was built solid, with hard muscle and a grip that was both confident and in charge. "Let's get you in the house."

"My, my!" The woman who had greeted them flipped the dish towel over her shoulder and hurried down the porch steps to reach Lainey Jo's other side. "What on earth happened?"

"Let's get her inside, Gramma Lou." The man had not loosened his grip on her, and Lainey Jo was glad. The ground moved beneath her feet, and she was quite sure he was all but carrying her on his hip into the cabin.

"Who are you, my dear?" The woman called "Gramma Lou" hurried to a stuffed chair covered in yellow velour from the eighties. She swiped a book from its seat and motioned for Lainey Jo to rest there.

"I'm Lainey Jo." It was all she was going to supply for now. WITSEC had been good about retaining her primary first name, but her last name was vastly different. She'd grown up as a Ludlow. That was a name that alone would bring raised eyebrows. The Ludlow name was known through the echelons of social circles down to the general population of the working class.

Gramma Lou hurried to a chest in the corner of the room, cracking open its lid. It reminded Lainey Jo of one of the antique travel trunks that people used to use on trains and steamers. She pulled out a patchwork quilt, hugging it in her arms as she crossed the room back toward Lainey Jo.

Unfolding it, she handed it to the man who still kept her on her feet while addressing Lainey Jo. "This quilt was my grandmother's. It's over a hundred years old, but it's guaranteed to give that warm embrace a soul needs when they're troubled."

Lainey Jo managed a weak smile.

"Bowen will help you settle in. I'll get my first aid kit." Gramma Lou hurried through a doorway into a side room.

Bowen. Her rescuer had a name. Lainey Jo met his eyes. They were blue, and they were troubled. She could see it the instant their eyes locked.

He eased her down into the chair, the cushion a blessed relief as she leaned her head back against it. Soon, the blanket was laid awkwardly on her lap, and Lainey Jo spared the man any more discomfort by pulling it up to her neck as she shivered. Her nerves were raw. Her head hurt. For that matter, her heart hurt—but she had no intention of going anywhere near that issue.

Bowen assessed her head wound. "A millimeter to the left and you'd be—" He bit off the word.

"Dead," Lainey Jo supplied for him. "I know." She closed her eyes.

"All righty," Gramma Lou half sang as she re-entered the room. It was a tiny living area. Two stuffed chairs angled to face a fireplace that was currently boasting a small but toasty fire. A crocheted afghan of greens and oranges was flung over the back of the sofa opposite Lainey Jo. She noted a table between them with a mason jar candle, a buffalo plaid flannel coaster and a bright purple coffee mug.

There was nothing aesthetically cohesive about this place. It was like a thrift store had supplied all the innards and yet, for the first time in the last hour, Lainey Jo felt a sense of security wash through her.

Gramma Lou opened her first aid kit and assessed Lainey Jo's head wound simultaneously. "It doesn't look to be deep. You're quite blessed to be alive."

The next several minutes were uncomfortable as Gramma Lou cleaned the head wound and then applied an antibiotic cream. She wrapped Lainey Jo's head with a bandage, then leaned back to assess her work. Gramma Lou's warm, brown eyes were empathetic. She patted Lainey Jo's leg. "You should rest." The older woman packed up her kit, turning her attention to Bowen. "And don't interrogate her. She's not one of your body snatches."

Confused, Lainey Jo glanced at Bowen. His mouth tightened at the term, but he maintained respect for his grandmother.

"I get it," he grumped.

Gramma Lou looked back at Lainey Jo, a small roll of her eyes an attempt to dismiss Bowen's severity. "Navy

SEALS are made of a different kind of mettle. Sometimes I have to remind him that not everyone is enemy personnel."

Lainey Jo still wasn't quite sure what Gramma Lou meant, but she mulled over the information that Bowen was a SEAL as Gramma Lou exited the room. She couldn't have picked a better vehicle to seek escape in. On the flip side, what was a navy SEAL doing in the foothills of the Bighorns with his grandmother? Was he retired? On leave?

She met Bowen's eyes. They were intense. He assessed her without subtlety. She noted a few tattoos on his forearms that disappeared beneath the rolled-up cuffs of his flannel shirt. One was a trident with an eagle.

Bowen followed the direction of her gaze and instead of offering any further explanation, he rolled his sleeve down, leaving the cuff unbuttoned. His palm scratched against his beard as he rubbed his chin. "No cops. No hospital. What are you hiding, Princess?"

The man had a thing for nicknames. Lainey Jo frowned.

He waited.

Yeah, she wasn't going to win the silent standoff. Lainey Jo had a feeling Bowen was well trained in the art of patience and observation.

"I'm not hiding anything." Her lie didn't even convince herself.

"Try again."

Lainey Jo drew in a steadying breath, turned away from Bowen's stern visage.

"Not going to talk?"

She swiveled her head back around, trying to ignore the throbbing headache that was building from the point of injury. "I can't."

Bowen's expression darkened. "You can't."

Lainey Jo swallowed a sudden need to cry. To expel the

emotion bottled within her from the fear of the afternoon's events. "I can't," she repeated.

Don't expose herself. That had been rule number one, the marshal assigned to her case had said. "Never give your real name. Don't try to contact your family or friends. As far as you're concerned, the life you lived doesn't exist anymore."

Granted, there were some allowances, Lainey Jo had discovered. For one, the FBI did offer to help her make contact with her parents once a year, if she needed. But she hadn't. The fear of Uncle Chris was real, and Lainey Jo had been worried he could issue retribution even from behind bars. She'd been right.

"WITSEC?"

Bowen's intuition stunned Lainey Jo. She stared at him. Words choked her throat. Everything in her wanted to tell him—well, tell him everything. But did she dare?

TWO

Bowen saw the fear in her eyes. He'd seen that type of fear before. What most people didn't realize was that there were different kinds of fear, and in his experience, this was one of the worst. This was fear that came from being trapped or cornered. When the hope of escape was such a thin line that the person wishing for it might get cut just walking along its sharp edge.

This was a mess. He could see that already. Someone had taken a shot at Lainey Jo, and she was fortunate they hadn't been very good at it. A good sniper wouldn't have missed, and she'd be dead. No. This was a wannabe. Someone who more likely practiced multiple methods of kill shots. Probably not military trained, and yet definitely not someone to be disregarded.

Bowen decided to give Lainey Jo some space. Not to mention, her reaction when he'd mentioned WITSEC was all he needed to know. She was in Witness Protection, obviously her cover had been blown, and now? He stood to the side of the front window that overlooked the gravel drive winding its way to the cabin through the woods. Scanning the area, he didn't see any movement. Nothing was out of place. But then, where most would find relief in that, Bowen only heightened his awareness. Quiet and serene all too often was the precursor before an ambush. The enemy could come out of nowhere. To underestimate them was to sign your own death certificate.

"Three years."

Lainey Jo's quivering voice broke the tense silence. Bowen didn't bother to look at her. He skirted the front door and moved to the window on the other side for a different vantage point. Besides, if she wanted to elaborate, she would. There was enough fear in her voice and eyes that Bowen knew it would only be a few more moments.

One.

Two.

Annnnd… "I've been in WITSEC for three years." …there she was.

Lainey Jo expanded on her original declaration. "I'm pretty sure they've found me."

Another quiver in her voice. Bowen's soft side—which was well controlled and compartmentalized—dared to rise to the surface. He glanced toward her. A tear was rolling down her cheek. He bit back a groan and instead abandoned his post for a tissue. Snatching one from the box on a cabinet, he crossed the room and handed it to Lainey Jo.

She looked up at him as he gave it to her. She had huge brown eyes like his Gramma Lou, only her irises were edged in velvet black lines, and her eyelashes were short and curled. If her hair were darker, she'd remind him of some of the women he'd seen in the Middle East.

Bowen blinked and gave his head a quick shake to clear his thoughts. This wasn't the Middle East. Still…he rerouted his pacing of the room to the one other window at the far end by the fireplace. It stared out into the woods. He fingered the gingham curtain just enough to give himself a clear line of sight.

"Who is after you?" No need to mince words.

"My uncle." Lainey Jo's response was quick and sure. "At least, I would guess that's who it is."

So much for the sure part. Bowen looked at her and appreciated the fact she held his gaze. "Why?"

"Because it was my testimony that put Uncle Chris behind bars."

Drugs? Money laundering? He wasn't going to waste time guessing. "What'd he do?"

Lainey Jo absently reached up to the bandage encircling her head. Her light brown hair was mussed and tangled, and it was obvious she was in some pain. "He—Uncle Chris—headed up a trafficking organization."

Bowen controlled his reaction, but the brevity of her declaration was not lost on him. Human trafficking. He'd dealt with a few ops that had entailed some of the worst. It was a disgusting line of work that only the lowest of humanity with the least amount of conscience could excel at.

And Lainey Jo had taken them on herself—family, no less.

Bowen's respect for her skyrocketed, even as he tugged his handgun from the holster at the small of his back. He checked the clip out of habit.

Lainey Jo's eyes widened, and Bowen offered her a slight shrug. "Can't be too careful then, can we?" It wasn't a question so much as a statement of fact. One that he knew he didn't need to offer Lainey Jo any further education on.

"I need to call—"

"Not a good idea," Bowen interrupted. "Calls can be traced."

"I know, but—" Lainey Jo adjusted herself on her seat. The sound of dishes clattering in the small kitchen off the main room of the cabin reminded them both that this would affect Gramma Lou as well. "I have a marshal assigned to me. Marshal Halloway. I need to get ahold of him and let him know what's happened."

"If he's any good, he already knows." Bowen knew his statement was unfair.

A grimace marred her pretty face. "He can get me to safety. The FBI can relocate me and—"

"Start all over again?" Bowen raised his brows in a slight challenge, not so much to Lainey Jo, but her circumstances. He'd seen people on the run for most of his career. He'd witnessed the toll it took on them, and the sickening truth was, it never lasted. Not really. Or maybe that was his jaded perspective from war speaking into his mind. "You really want to do that?"

"What choice do I have?" Lainey Jo's question was direct and demanded an answer.

Bowen appreciated that. He contemplated it for a moment. "Fight back."

Lainey Jo issued a small laugh of disbelief. "I'm not a navy SEAL. Besides, Uncle Chris is supposed to be in prison. The entire organization was dismantled. I don't even know who or what exactly I'd be fighting against."

At ease for the moment that the perimeter of the cabin was secure, Bowen sank onto a chair opposite Lainey Jo. He tapped his fingers on his knees, considering the options. She was right. There weren't many, and the rational next step was to make contact with the marshal. But not here. He'd prefer not to bring Gramma Lou any deeper into all this by making her home their base.

"Let's take a trip." He pushed off the chair.

Lainey Jo eyed him warily.

"We'll take my truck to the ridge. You can get a signal there. I have a burner phone, so we'll use that."

"You have a burner phone?" Lainey Jo asked in disbelief.

Bowen didn't find it necessary—or any of her business, really—to know all the means of protection and safety he had in place. It was natural to him. He sidestepped her question. "We have to be smart about this." He recalled she'd already used his regular phone shortly after she'd jumped into his vehicle. "Did you try calling the marshal earlier?"

"When I jumped in your truck?" Lainey Jo verified. At his nod, she gave him an affirmative. "Yes. He didn't answer."

"Okay." So there was a slim possibility the call could have been intercepted and whoever was after Lainey Jo already had a pin on his location via his phone. But then, her hopping into his truck had been so random, it was doubtful whoever was after her was that organized and prepared with tech to do that. But Bowen didn't like to take chances. "Let me clear the area and then we'll take off." His Sig felt familiar in his hand. Comfortable. An old buddy that he knew he could count on—assuming he was on his game.

This time, he had to be. Lainey Jo's life depended on him. At least until he delivered her into the protection of Marshal Halloway. Then he could walk away and return to Gramma Lou's and try to forget it all. Forget it all, along with everything else.

The truck bounced on the road, and even though it was a paved highway, that didn't mean there weren't divots and dips. Lainey Jo's head felt every one of them. A sideways glance at Bowen, and she could see that he was focused on their surroundings and not aware of her pounding headache.

Gramma Lou had grumbled as Bowen led Lainey Jo from her cabin. "She's in no shape to be out gallivanting with you, Bowen Mays." But they were hardly "gallivanting," and Bowen's response had been to merely drop a kiss on his grandmother's cheek and give her a backward wave as he headed to his truck.

"That boy." Gramma Lou clucked her tongue and then gave Lainey Jo a conspiratorial look of empathy. "Hang in there, sweet one."

And she was. For dear life. Literally.

Lainey Jo clenched and unclenched her hands in her lap. Bowen wasn't talkative, and his serious demeanor was intimidating if not downright unfriendly. Yet Lainey Jo couldn't help but notice his profile and appreciate it. He was solid, everything about his body firm and compact. His hair was cut short enough to try to control the curl, and yet just long enough at the nape of his neck for the curl to rebel. It was brown but tinged with red, and with the sunlight bouncing off of it, it looked chestnut in color. Irish. He had to have Irish blood in him. The smattering of freckles that mixed with his whiskers and into his beard told her that. In another life—or a romance novel—he'd be the epitome of a swoon-worthy Alpha male hero. Lainey Jo had never been attracted to alphas. In another life, she'd have preferred the professor type. Someone bookish, predictable and precise. Like her father. Scott Ludlow was everything opposite of her Uncle Chris. Uncle Chris was alpha.

Lainey Jo shifted her attention from Bowen and back onto the road. The Bighorn Mountains were beautiful. Peaceful. Forests of Ponderosa pine stretched for miles, and here on the highway, she could see across the valley like a bird perched high over the world. It was comforting to be above it all. It felt safe.

"The minute you feel safe," Bowen interrupted her thoughts as though he read them, "you're not. We'll stop at a pull-off about a mile up ahead. Make the call to Marshal Halloway, but be aware. Stay near the vehicle. Don't stand out in the open."

"I don't think—"

"Always think." Bowen cut off her words, and Lainey Jo pursed her lips, irritated.

"Are you always this blunt?" she couldn't help but ask. She made herself feel better for her direct question by swapping out the word "rude" for "blunt."

Bowen shot her a glance and then turned his eyes back onto the road. "Well, Princess, yes, I am."

And he was unapologetic as well.

Lainey Jo struggled to maintain her composure. The sooner she could reach Marshal Halloway and meet up with him, the better. On one hand, she had a modicum of security considering Bowen's military background. But on the other hand, the more she got to know of him, the more he grated on her sensitive nerves.

Bowen steered the truck onto a pull-out that jutted off the highway and curved to give passersby a wide view of the landscape. Another car was parked, and Bowen held up his hand and shot her a warning glance. "Hold up. Let me check it out."

Lainey Jo suppressed her desire to roll her eyes. He might be taking this a little too far. There was no way that whoever was after her could possibly know where she was now. She had no trackers, no phone, Bowen was a legitimate stranger to her, so unless they'd been followed—and nothing gave that impression—she was probably safer than she had been in a while.

Bowen's stance was casual as he exited the truck and meandered to the edge of the pull-out. Large boulders lined the drop-off, and he stood with his hands on his hips as though enjoying the view. A woman and a child appeared from inside the car, and she smiled at Bowen as she wrestled the toddler into submission. Another woman was in the driver's seat. Bowen seemed to give his assessment of them no less attention than had they been males. He looked over his shoulder at Lainey Jo and gave a clipped nod.

Good. She was anxious to call Marshal Halloway. The fact he hadn't answered earlier bothered her, but then, there had been a time or two over the last three years when he hadn't. She clutched the phone Bowen had given her in her hand and climbed out of the truck to get a better signal. Per his instructions, she stayed by the door.

The air was crisp, and the breeze ruffled her hair at her shoulders. The bandage Gramma Lou had wrapped around her head was still in place, and Lainey Jo noticed one of the women from the car give her a second glance. Ignoring them, she quickly dialed the marshal. Bowen continued to look over the valley, but she noticed he was always turning to look behind them and around them.

The phone rang, and a familiar voice answered. "Halloway."

Thank You, Lord! Lainey Jo sent up her silent prayer and immediately launched into the report of the day's events. Halloway had a series of questions for her, and then, within minutes, they arranged a place and time to meet up.

"We'll get you into a safe house," Halloway concluded, "and then go from there."

"Thank you." Lainey Jo's gratitude was followed by an involuntary shiver. "I—" She needed to let him know about Bowen. "I have a friend bringing me. He—he's helped me stay safe today."

There was a short pause, as if Halloway was digesting the news that someone else was involved in her situation. He asked for Bowen's name.

"Bowen Mays," she supplied, trying out his full name for the first time.

"Be cautious, Lainey Jo." Halloway's instruction included Bowen as much as it did the unknown threats that hunted her. "Get to the meetup as soon as you can."

Ending the call, Lainey Jo met Bowen's inquiring stare. "He wants to meet up in Dayton." She gave Bowen the exact location—a gas station in a small town in the valley near the pass to head into the mountains. "Halloway wants us to be there in an hour."

"Great." Bowen's affirmation was quick, and he motioned toward the truck. "Let's go. It'll take us about that to get there."

Lainey Jo crawled back into the truck, blinking repeatedly as her headache increased, causing a pulsating throb to squeeze like a band around her head.

Bowen appeared to notice her wince as he started his truck. Lainey Jo was surprised as his icy blue eyes softened and the lines around his eyes relaxed with an expression of understanding. "Head wounds are beasts. Why don't you close your eyes and try to get some rest?"

Lainey Jo had no reticence in agreeing. She wrapped her arms around herself and her seat belt and leaned her head back against the headrest. For now, the Bighorns offered her protection with their seclusion. And Bowen. Bowen offered her protection too. Something in her gut told her she could trust the navy SEAL—no matter his history and whatever secret pain she could see lurking behind the ocean of awareness in his eyes. She could see it because she saw the same secret pain in her eyes. The pain of betrayal from Uncle Chris. The pain of knowing that, regardless of her privileged and idealized upbringing, her parents had so readily let her enter WITSEC with no contact even being attempted in three years. It was like an extra wound to an already raw heart. She was alone, hurt and afraid, angry at herself for giving up her uncle while at the same time, before God, sure it had been the right decision.

But that's how secret wounds bled. Slowly and quietly, and the only one who noticed was the wounded one. Until someone came along who messed with the homemade bandages.

Lainey Jo glanced at Bowen and then closed her eyes.

She had the feeling, if given enough time, Bowen would do more than disturb her secret pain. He would expose it.

Something was off. Bowen could feel it the instant he saw the gas station that lay on the outskirts of Dayton. It made sense that it wasn't smack in the center of the small town—they wouldn't want to draw a lot of attention. But no cars were at the station. Not even a vehicle that might belong to the attendant working there. To the north were acres of fields, ranch fencing and at least a hundred head of cattle that dotted the landscape. To the south, and across the barren highway, was a bar that wouldn't be open until later that evening, its parking lot also empty. They were the only two public buildings on this stretch. The other structures were at least an eighth of a mile east toward Dayton, and they were outbuildings that probably housed machinery and ranch materials. A small house was tucked in between them, but the commercial sign that was perched over its roof appeared—at least from this distance—to be an advertisement.

Lainey Jo stirred beside him. She'd fallen asleep on the way. He could tell by the soft breathing and the way her body had relaxed—relaxed into *him*. With no center console between them, she'd slid on the bench seat until her head rested on his shoulder. He'd not bothered to move her. The girl needed her zzz's. He wasn't about to admit that the vulnerability in her trust awakened something inside him. Bowen had no intention of exploring that feeling, and now, with trepidation building, it was also the last thing on his mind.

"C'mon, Chicken Little." He shook his shoulder, and Lainey Jo wakened with a start. "The sky is falling." His declaration caused Lainey Jo to jerk upright, a panicked expression washing over her face.

"What's wrong?" Her eyes were wide, taking in their surroundings.

A twinge of guilt for scaring her nagged at Bowen. He hadn't meant for her to panic, just to awaken and be alert. He didn't apologize as the truck continued its journey toward the station. There wasn't time to worry about feelings and intentions.

"Keep your head on a swivel," he instructed Lainey Jo. "The place is deserted."

"Shouldn't it be?" Her question confirmed to Bowen that any past meetups had been in more obscure locations.

"Empty isn't a good sign. You want some movement. Some signs of life." Bowen squinted against the daylight as the sun moved from behind the clouds. The turn into the station was just up ahead. He scanned the area as best as he could. There were plenty of places for someone to be lying in wait to attack. There were also plenty of vantage points if Lainey Jo's would-be killer wanted to try their hand at a sniper's rifle again.

"Halloway said he'd be here." A thread of worry laced Lainey Jo's voice. So, she had noticed the lack of vehicles too.

"Yeah. Did he say what he'd be driving?" Bowen asked,

turning the steering wheel and slowing to a crawl. The truck's tires crunched on gravel as they rolled into the station.

"A black Suburban," Lainey Jo replied.

"Subtle. Not at all predictable." Bowen couldn't disguise the sarcasm as he spoke his thoughts aloud.

A *ping* sounded as a bullet ricocheted off the gravel in front of the truck.

"Get down!" Bowen shoved Lainey Jo onto the seat with one hand as he wrenched the steering wheel and swerved. He pressed his foot on the gas, causing gravel to spin as his tires transferred from the gravel drive onto the station's asphalt lot.

Lainey Jo crouched down in the seat, her hand brushing his leg as she tried to hang on. Bowen swerved around the gas pumps, the truck tires squealing as he rounded the western corner of the station.

"What do we do?" Lainey Jo's cry was desperate, and one Bowen wished he knew the answer to. He didn't like this place. There wasn't much to take shelter in, and he wasn't at all sure that, if they exited his truck, the station was unlocked and open for them to position in.

"The gunshot came from the direction of the bar across the road." Bowen slammed on the brakes, throwing his right arm over the seat Lainey Jo was ducking in, and twisting to look over his shoulder and assess the situation. "I think we're good here for now. I'm going to see if we can get into the station."

"What if it was the sniper?" Lainey Jo shot him a frightened look, and Bowen hesitated for only a margin of a second.

"Doesn't matter who it is—they're shooting at us. Whoever fired is maybe a couple of hundred yards away. I want to know where your marshal is!" Bowen was fast beginning to question Marshal Halloway's choice of meetup and, frankly, even his trustworthiness. If a shooter had found Lainey Jo in her home, and now here? That meant someone on the inside was feeding the shooter information, if not the shooter himself.

"Stay down and give me a minute." Bowen edged from the driver's seat of the truck, bent at the waist, his gun drawn. The gas station door was just around the corner from where he'd stopped the truck, but it was also right in line with the shooter. There had to be a back entrance. Bowen sprinted for the building, taking shelter behind an ice tank. No more shots fired, and while some might take that as a relief, it worried Bowen. More than likely, the shooter was repositioning. They would have the truck—and Lainey Jo—in sight in no time.

He was left with two options. Find a way inside, call for backup from local authorities, and hope that Marshal Halloway showed up also as a good guy. Or hop back in the truck and make for the mountains with Lainey Jo in tow.

Bowen moved forward a few steps and eased his way around the corner to the back of the station. He froze.

A man sprawled on the ground, a growing pool of blood beneath him. A Stetson hat had been knocked from his head and had rolled several feet away. It was apparent from the bullet hole wound in the man's temple that not only was he dead, but he'd been shot by someone who had no qualms about pulling a trigger up close and personal. The flash of a star on his chest told Bowen all he needed to know.

Marshal Halloway had been ambushed, and he was dead. He'd be no help now.

Another shot rang out, and this time Bowen stiffened, spinning back in the direction of his truck. The connection of bullet to metal sent adrenaline through him. But it was the piercing scream from Lainey Jo that chilled him to the bone.

A prayer rose inside of him—something Bowen hadn't done since the last time he'd heard a scream like that. And the last time, prayer had failed him—just like he'd failed his mission. He wasn't going to let that happen again.

THREE

"Get down! Get down!"

Bowen's command was emphasized by the pounding of his hand against the side of the truck.

Another bullet zinged through the air and hit the gravel at Bowen's feet just as he swung open the door and dove into the truck. His arm slammed into Lainey Jo as she curled in the passenger seat.

"That's the worst wanna-be sniper I've ever seen!" Bowen's exclamation might have been a little funny were they not being shot at.

"What do we do?" Lainey Jo was completely helpless and she hated the feeling. Being pinned down by even an untalented shooter was never something on her list of things to experience. The split second of guilt that she'd dragged Bowen into her mess sliced through her as he hunkered over the steering wheel, keeping his head down, and turning the key in the ignition.

Another shot. This time, the bullet pierced the windshield.

Lainey Jo couldn't control her cry. She clapped her hands over her mouth, trying not to be a distraction as glass pelted her.

The truck roared to life, and Bowen pressed the gas

pedal with his booted foot. They lurched forward, and he lifted his head just enough to know to turn the wheel to a sharp left. They careened onto the road and, in a few moments, had left the scene behind in a cloud of dust.

Lainey Jo hadn't lifted her head yet. She hugged the passenger door, her body hunched so it stayed lower than the dash and as far below the side window as she could get.

Bowen reached up as if he were going to touch the bullet hole in his windshield, but he dropped his hand as if he thought better of it.

"Yeah," he muttered. "The shooter ain't no SEAL."

Lainey Jo hesitated, then peeked over the dash. Trees and fence lines flew past the window as the truck sped away from Dayton.

"You can sit up," Bowen stated.

Lainey Jo did so, trying to hide her shaking hands by tucking them under her thighs. "Marshal Halloway?" She knew the answer even before Bowen confirmed it.

"Dead."

He seemed to be the king of punchy sentences, but at the moment, Lainey Jo couldn't blame him. She'd turned his entire life upside down and almost gotten him killed.

It was apparent he was very aware of where they were and whether or not they had a tail. Even now, he didn't bother to give her much attention, and instead, his eyes did a continual sweep from the driver's side mirror, to rearview, to passenger side, and even the occasional physical twisting to look over his shoulder.

"We're in the clear."

At his statement, Lainey Jo pulled her hands from beneath her legs and managed to fold them in her lap. This was all going south so fast, and she had dragged this man into her troubles.

Bowen glanced at her. "You okay?"

"Yeah." She nodded. At least she could pretend she was. "Just shook up."

"You'd be dead if that shooter had any training."

Lainey Jo couldn't help but stare at Bowen, her eyes wide as she bit her bottom lip in nervous deliberation as to whether he was right or not. But who was she to question his expertise? It wasn't as if she knew anything about shooters, being shot at, or guns, for that matter.

"That's twice they've tried to take you out."

"They?" Lainey Jo tried to remember if she'd told Bowen she thought there had been two men earlier. One who was the shooter, and the other who had ransacked her apartment and then chased after her.

Bowen nodded, keeping his attention on the road and the mirrors. "The marshal was shot at close range. One gunshot to his temple."

"Oh." Lainey Jo could only acknowledge Bowen's observation.

"Snipers go for center mass."

She hadn't asked, but now she knew. It was more than she wanted to know, if she were honest.

"And, this sniper must not have had a spotter."

Lainey Jo eyed Bowen who turned right onto a narrow road that led deeper into the wilderness and off the main highway. "A spotter?" she inquired.

"Yeah. They're the ones who calculate range and call wind. The guy shooting at us? He was long-distance, yeah, but he was making quick, irregular shots. He's not an actual sniper."

"Then why shoot from far away? Why not have the second guy just ambush me?"

"That's what I want to know," Bowen agreed.

The guy was intense, that was for sure. Lainey Jo studied him for a long second. His jaw was set, his eyes like steel, and he gripped the steering wheel with corded hands. He was powerful and compact, and he seemed…*alive*. As though somehow he was in his element while Lainey Jo wanted to curl up and hide in the deepest, darkest corner. Maybe that's what it took to be a navy SEAL. A passion for danger, an intoxication with adrenaline, a need to not be still and not live an average life of general safety.

"The fact is, someone wants you dead. Bad enough to send two people after you. From the looks of it, one isn't afraid of up close and personal. The other is more hands-off."

"What does that even mean?" Lainey Jo tried to wrap her head around Bowen's observations.

He adjusted his grip on the steering wheel as the truck bounced over a rut in the road. "Whoever has taken shots at you from a distance—I'd guess they're either hired or don't want any chance of being tied to your death. It's why they're opting for long-range—granted, that's also what has saved you. The other guy—"

"The one who shot Marshal Halloway?" Lainey Jo questioned.

"Yeah. They're invested in this. They're either close to the person behind it, or they *are* the person behind it. And they don't have complete confidence in their partner, for obvious reasons, being the fact you're still alive."

"Someone was chasing me when I ran from my apartment," Lainey Jo offered. "It was a man, but I didn't see his face."

"Did he say anything? Was there anything recognizable about him?"

Lainey Jo forced herself to think back to earlier in the

day when she'd crawled across her apartment's floor, then sprinted from the building. The man had been average height, dressed in black, with a black stocking cap pulled low over his features. She shook her head. "He just looked like any normal man," she supplied. "He was a man dressed in black."

"That's normal?"

She didn't miss Bowen's sideways glance.

"Well, I meant the average-looking part."

"Could it have been your uncle?"

"My Uncle Chris is in prison," Lainey Jo said.

"You sure about that?" A sideways glance of doubt was enough to make Lainey Jo's stomach flip with anxiety.

"Yes." But was she really sure? The marshals would have told her if he'd gotten out, wouldn't they? Early release? No. No judge on earth would have released him.

"He could be directing things from prison." Bowen turned down an even narrower road. This one was dirt, and trees brushed against the side of the truck as he slowly maneuvered it. Lainey Jo had no idea where they were, but it was more than apparent, Bowen did.

At Lainey Jo's questioning stare, Bowen filled her in. "I'm taking you to a safe house."

"You have one of those?" That was unexpected. Lainey Jo considered the implications. "What are *you* hiding from?"

He shot her a glance. "Nothing. I just like to be prepared."

The trees had grown thicker, and the road had become more of a trail. Some of the ruts in the road were deep enough to tilt the truck to the left, and Lainey Jo gripped the doorframe as if it would somehow hold her secure.

She couldn't have asked God for a better-qualified protector on one hand, but on the other—Lainey Jo dared one last glance at Bowen Mays—there was a side to him that seemed dangerous. There was also something in his expression that she caught when he thought she wasn't looking. It reminded her of a stray dog that had lived outside of their complex in Paris when she was a kid. It was tough, rough around the edges, and whenever Lainey Jo had sat in her window to watch it, it was also fighting off bigger dogs, humans who thought to abuse it, and once, even a dog catcher. But when no one was near it, the dog's tail would tuck between his legs, his ears would droop, and a sadness fell over him. His toughness was a cover for a hurting puppy inside.

Maybe that was an unfair comparison to Bowen Mays, navy SEAL and now her protector. But Lainey Jo couldn't help it. The similarities between them evoked a compassion in her. Even a trust. She supposed it could very well be misplaced. Not to mention, anyone would think she had lost her mind if she told them she'd chosen to trust Bowen Mays because of a stray alley dog she'd watched in Paris when she was eight.

Still, she had little choice but to trust him now. With Marshal Halloway dead, who did she have left?

Lainey Jo looked at the cabin—shack, rather—that was built in a valley, its slanted, clapboard porch facing a wide stream that rolled over rocks and swirled in clear water pools. With the back of the place butted against the rocky hillside, covered in lodgepole pines and shrubs, it created a secure covering. Across the creek, a similar cliffside rose, making it clear there was a primary way in and out by following the flow of the water.

"I'm not a fan of the idea of someone up on the hill able

to pick us off, but we don't have much of a choice at the moment." Bowen opened the door to the cabin, pushing inward and revealing a very simplistic layout inside. "This is my buddy's hunting shack. I'd rather you stay here than at Gramma Lou's."

Lainey Jo couldn't argue with his reasoning. If they returned to the woman's homey place, they would also be bringing potential danger to her front door. Lainey Jo didn't want that. Not at all.

She entered the cabin as Bowen stood aside for her to go ahead of him. "Thank you." She turned, facing him. "I'm sorry for bringing you into this."

Bowen followed behind her and shut the door. He skirted her and went to the windows, drawing the cords off canvas curtains meant to help keep out the light rather than look pretty. They fell into place, offering a modicum of privacy.

She took a moment to survey the room. A table sat to the left, with a long counter, a kitchen sink, and, toward the back of the room, a cast-iron woodstove. A pair of antlers hung on the wall, the only bit of decor that managed to make the kitchen area look homey. Two wooden-framed chairs made up the living space, with plaid cushions for the backs and seats. There was an end table with a few books on it. She recognized the titles.

Great Expectations.

The Art of War.

Charlotte's Web.

Lainey Jo hadn't expected that last one. She glanced at Bowen, who was watching her.

"It's my friend's book. He likes animals."

"Oh." She didn't quite know what to say to that, as it was usually considered a book for kids and Charlotte was an arachnid, but she let it go.

He didn't respond any further, but instead waved his arm toward where Lainey Jo stood. "You can have the bed." He pointed to a cot at the far corner. "Keep the curtains drawn. No lights at night."

"Where are you going to be?" She hesitated, half wishing he'd stay and half hoping he'd leave. She wasn't sure which would be better.

Bowen didn't directly answer. "There are MREs in the cupboard if you get hungry."

"MREs?"

His eyes rested on her, and Lainey Jo almost wished she hadn't asked. It was disconcerting to be the focal point of his intense, blue assessment. "Ready to eat meals."

"Oh." She found herself saying that a lot today.

When he didn't say anything, Lainey Jo tried to offer a resolution to today's chaos. "If I can get in contact with Marshal Halloway's supervisor, I—"

"No." Bowen cut her off.

"No?"

"Whoever is after you knew we were planning to meet up with the marshal in Dayton. They were there waiting for him, and I'm sure you called him on a secure line, so that doesn't bode well."

Lainey Jo nodded, assuming Bowen was right. Her stomach knotted. "But if they knew—" She stopped, the weight of her realization slamming into her. "Someone in the marshals told them we were meeting Marshal Halloway?"

Bowen shrugged. "Maybe. Maybe not. But if there's a leak somewhere, we need to be very cautious. Checking in with the wrong person could expose you. Regardless, until we have some time to think and plan, you shouldn't go anywhere. I'm going to head out and get some more supplies, and then I'll be back."

"I'm supposed to just stay here? Alone?" It wasn't that she doubted him. Fine. Yes, she did. She was stuck out in the wilderness, in a stranger's cabin, with a stranger offering protection and giving orders, and she was uneasy to say the least.

"Do you want me to take you home?" he countered.

Well, that wasn't funny.

"No."

"Smart. Like I said, I'll be back later. So you won't be alone for long."

"Where will you sleep?" Lainey Jo couldn't help but ask.

The look Bowen shot her made her think he was taken aback by her question, but not because she was concerned about sleeping arrangements, and more so because she'd brought up the concept of sleep at all.

"I don't sleep," he stated. "I'll be out there." Bowen pointed toward the door. "Keeping watch."

"Alone?" Lainey Jo breathed. There was no way one man could stand guard around the clock for long.

His mouth tipped in a slight smile, and he gave her a little wink. She hadn't expected that, and it did something to her nerves that was different than the terrified sparks that had been shooting off inside of her.

"Don't worry about me. I'm not alone."

With those cryptic words, he left her standing in the middle of the cabin, the door closing behind him. His footsteps sounded on the porch, and then Lainey Jo heard them returning. The door opened, and he poked his head back in, his eyes drilling into her. "Don't even *think* of leaving the cabin. Stay put, stay low."

Lainey Jo shook her head. "I won't."

And then he was gone. She was alone. The Bighorn

Mountains, in which Lainey Jo hid, brought a modicum of safety.

She hoped.

Bowen paid close attention to any vehicles around him or any sense that he might be followed. The fact that his gut told him he was in the clear was a good thing, but if Zeke ever became recognizable as the truck that had driven off with Lainey Jo Whatever-her-WITSEC-last-name-was in it, he'd be in trouble. Thankfully, it seemed like at least a quarter of the truck-owning population had beat-up, gray pickups in Wyoming. So he was counting on maintaining his obscurity.

Lainey Jo. Bowen tried not to focus on the woman hiding out in the hunting shack that his old teammate, Pax, owned and made available to him. The problem was, Bowen could tell that Lainey Jo wasn't skilled at anything other than average life. She had no sense of what was around her. There was no apparent awareness of vantage points and areas someone hunting her could hide, and she didn't even seem to have a strong understanding of what to do when her life was threatened.

It didn't help that her face was all but emblazoned in his mind. He couldn't shake it, and he couldn't shake her. She reminded him too much of the past. His past. His failure to provide a safe evacuation for a woman who had needed him. The mission had failed. *He* had failed. There were no excuses when you were a SEAL. You did your job. Except, he hadn't. Bowen had spent the last year praying that God would give him some sort of respite from the guilt he carried, but instead, God had seen fit to drop another rescue in his lap.

He didn't have the option to just wipe his hands of her.

That wasn't in his DNA either. So here he was, making plans to keep the woman safe in a rugged environment, and in a situation he knew next to nothing about. That needed to change. Fast. Whoever had taken out the marshal overseeing Lainey Jo's case was serious, and this wasn't going to just go away. It would have been nice to hand Lainey Jo over to US Marshals and walk away, but at this point, Bowen didn't have confidence that was even safe. Not until—or if—he could find out how someone had gotten the drop on Marshal Halloway before Bowen and Lainey Jo even had time to get down the mountain to meet up with him. It hadn't slipped past Bowen that the marshal's vehicle had been missing when they'd arrived. It was probable an assailant had stolen it to get away fast. But regardless, whoever they were up against was not just playing games. They were deadly serious.

He pulled Zeke to a stop outside of Gramma Lou's place. The front door was open as he hiked up the short path. He preferred her location for safety purposes. They weren't cut off by mountainous terrain on either side like the hunting cabin Lainey Jo was at. But he couldn't bring her back here. He could not put Gramma Lou at risk any more than she already might be.

"Where is Lainey Jo?" she asked immediately upon Bowen's entrance.

He sniffed the air, smelling her beef stew. His stomach growled, but he ignored it, opting to hike to a gun cabinet on the far wall. Bowen didn't miss Gramma Lou's worried expression.

"What's going on, Bowen?" She perched her hands on her hips.

He made fast work of pulling out a black canvas duffel

and filling it with ammunition. "She's in a bit of trouble," was all he supplied.

"Well, I figured that!" Gramma Lou approached him, crossing her arms over her chest. She was no elderly woman. No, she was not. Bowen knew he got a lot of his inner constitution from his grandmother, and not a little of her physical prowess. For seventy-four, Gramma Lou was fit and spry and her own force of nature. "Don't you cut me out of this, Bowen Mays."

He paused, bent over the duffel bag, and lifted his eyes. "I'm keeping you safe."

"Aha!" A knowing smile creased her face. "I'm in the mood for a good tussle." She clucked her tongue. "I'll have my shotgun loaded."

Bowen couldn't help but chuckle, and he stood to full height, staring down at the woman who had all but raised him. "There are at least two of them."

"I can handle that." Her stubborn chin lifted.

He sure loved her. Bowen reached for his grandmother on a rare impulse and pulled her into a gruff hug. He set her back and away from him then, holding her upper arms lightly. "They're dangerous, Gram. And they're wild cards."

"What does that mean?" Gramma Lou's eyes flashed with worry.

"It means," Bowen resumed packing his duffel bag, "that they're unpredictable. I don't know what their endgame is yet."

"To get to Lainey Jo?" she supplied.

"More likely to *get* Lainey Jo. But why? What changed? What's influencing them? And if they're stopped, will more come in their place?" Bowen zipped the duffel bag and lifted it to a chair. "There are too many variables at the moment. I need to gather the intel and then come up with a plan. Until then, I need to keep Lainey Jo alive, and *you* need to stay out of the way and not pick fights with hostiles."

"I didn't say I'd pick a fight, but I won't run away, either." The ferocity in Gramma Lou's eyes made Bowen proud. And it heightened his concern. In a way, Lainey Jo was like his grandmother, in that both of them had no idea the real threat of men on a mission to kill. There was no giving up. There was no taking a break. The hunter would push forward, and in reality, life became a ticking time bomb until the threat was defused.

Bowen dropped a kiss on her head, and Gramma Lou batted him away. "Enough of that sentimental nonsense. That's not like you at all!" She reached up and gripped his chin, his scruff making a scratching sound beneath her fingers. Gramma Lou assessed him carefully, her eyes narrowing.

"This isn't because of *her*, is it? You're feeling some penance is due, and that's why you're getting involved now with Lainey Jo?"

Bowen swallowed hard. Gramma Lou knew everything that had happened to the American woman he'd failed to save. She also knew that guilt drove a lot of his choices in life.

"I'm involved because that's what I do," Bowen reassured her, as much as to convince himself. It wasn't penance, because there was nothing he could do that would ever be great enough to make up for what he'd allowed to happen. "Lainey Jo needs my help. Period."

"And you're going to get Paxton to help you, yes?" Gramma Lou referred to his buddy and teammate who had followed him to the mountains of Wyoming after they'd both been discharged after the last mission.

Medical discharge for both of them.

One of them could still hold his head up high, though, and that SEAL wasn't Bowen.

FOUR

It'd been an hour and she was going stir-crazy. Not to mention, if the shooter had followed them to the cabin, she was alone with no means of self-defense. Lainey Jo leaned forward in the wooden-framed chair and the remarkably comfortable plaid cushions. If she were smart, she would look for a weapon to protect herself with. Far be it from her to leave her welfare up to a navy SEAL. Not that she could compete, but she could at least *try* to appear competent.

Lainey Jo leapt up from her seat and surveyed the cabin. The cot in the corner looked passable as a place to sleep, but she highly doubted she'd be able to use the pillow to smother an assailant. Well…? No. She shifted her assessment to the end table. Next to the books was a pencil. She'd watched a movie once where a guy had killed a villain by jabbing the pencil into his neck. It was an option. But not one she was sure she had the stomach for. Still, Lainey Jo reached down and picked up the pencil, carrying it to the table and setting it down.

The kitchen had to have more options. It was a kitchen, after all. She opened a drawer and eyed the utensils.

"Seriously? Plastic?" Lainey Jo lifted a plastic knife. That would be as effective on a human as it would be trying to carve an apple. She tossed it back into the drawer.

Closing that drawer, she tugged out the only other one. A silicone spoon, a carrot peeler, a meat thermometer and a set of measuring spoons. Considering the lack of a pantry, she wondered why Bowen's friend even had these items at the cabin at all.

She opened a cupboard. Plates. Bowls. "I guess I could throw them at someone."

There were a few washcloths and a dish towel. A box of matches. A supply of plastic baggies stuffed into a plastic container that had probably once housed potato salad from a deli.

She was striking out on the weapons front.

Lainey Jo eyed the pencil and then decided praying was a better option. If God could just keep the bad guys away, at least until Bowen returned, she'd be so grateful!

The cast-iron woodstove in the corner grabbed her attention and Lainey Jo moved toward it. She opened the firebox. It was empty. The stove door opened with a clatter. Very clean, but also very empty.

"There's not even a cast-iron skillet."

Above the stovetop, there was a warming oven. Lainey Jo grasped the metal handle and pulled it open.

She froze.

Well, that was unexpected.

Reaching inside, Lainey pulled out a handgun. It was holstered, but she had a very strong feeling it was loaded. A momentary sense of relief washed through her. She'd shot a handgun a few times. A friend in high school had enjoyed going to a shooting range, and Lainey Jo had gone along with her. She wasn't sure she could remember how to shoot it, and if she did, she was certain she wouldn't be a good shot.

But a gun was better than a pencil.

Wasn't it?

* * *

Lainey Jo pushed the curtain back just an inch so she could peek through the cabin window. She'd heard the vehicle approaching, and her emotions swung wildly. For the last couple of hours, she'd huddled on the cot in the corner of the cabin, replaying the day's events as dusk began to set in. The more she considered them, the more frightened she became, and the more alert she was to every little noise and bump. She kept the handgun by her side and had examined it enough to think she knew how to shoot it.

Lainey Jo wished Bowen back with a fury while at the same time, she was riddled with guilt for pulling the man into her circle of trouble. The poor guy had been trying to buy groceries! A woman hopping into his truck with killers on her heels was probably not on Bowen's list of things to expect for the day. And yet, here she was, in a cabin hidden miles from the main road as if it had been provided just for her.

It had been, she realized, and while Lainey Jo breathed a prayer of thanks that God had seen fit to bring her to a place of safety, she also grieved over the fact that a half hour away, Marshal Halloway's body was probably being found and retrieved in a body bag.

The marshal was dead. Her primary contact for Witness Protection, and now Bowen seemed to think she couldn't trust the US Marshals. That seemed ridiculous, but then, if Uncle Chris had a contact in the department who fed him information, Bowen was right. Any contact with the marshals would seal her fate for being found.

Now, her curiosity to see who was at the wheel of the vehicle was met with relief when she saw the gray, rusted pickup with Bowen at the wheel. Lainey Jo let the curtain fall back into place, clutching the handgun in her right hand. She moved to the front door, unlocked and opened it.

"Never do that." Bowen's clipped greeting was followed by his abrupt entrance into the cabin.

Lainey Jo felt his scolding like a heavy pit in her stomach. "Do what?"

"Unlock the door and open it without being aware of your surroundings." He dumped a black canvas duffel bag on top of the bare kitchen table.

"I was aware. I knew it was you." He could scold her all he wanted, but she had to stick up for herself at some point. Lainey Jo kept the handgun at her side, pointing down to the floor, and eyed him. "I'm not that dumb."

Bowen set a paper bag stuffed with goods next to the duffel. "What if the sniper's up there on the ridgeline? Opening the door gave him the perfect opportunity to pick you off."

Lainey Jo squirmed as Bowen leveled a blue stare on her. "But, you said he was a horrible sniper." It was all she could think to say.

Throwing his words back at Bowen made his face crack into a smile. Well, now, *that* did things to Lainey Jo's stomach that were entirely different than what she had been experiencing. This wasn't fear. This was the visceral reaction of a vulnerable female standing in front of a fine specimen of a navy SEAL who now smiled. The creases in his cheeks? The bearded scruff on his jaw? The deep-set eyes and dark brows? In another time and place, Lainey Jo would have been at a loss for words because he was the epitome of attractive. But now? Okay, fine. She was at a loss for words now, and it simply wasn't a good time to find herself palpitating like a lovestruck schoolgirl.

"'Kay. You got me." He rested his hands at his waist.

"But in the future, I'll knock like this." He rapped a pattern on the wooden table. "That's the cue that it's safe to open the door. Got it, Tadpole?"

Tadpole? She liked it better when he called her "Princess."

Fine.

Lainey Jo nodded.

"Good." Bowen turned to the paper bag and removed some items. "Gramma Lou made sure you're supplied," he said. "Warm socks and apparently—" he held up a pair of flannel bottoms "—she felt it was important you had pajamas."

God bless Gramma Lou.

"And a sweatshirt." Bowen unexpectedly tossed the articles her way, and Lainey Jo tried to catch them with her left hand. They fell to the floor.

Bowen spotted the gun in her right hand. His brows went up and then almost in the same instant, turned down in a scowl. He cleared the distance between them and extracted the gun from her hand.

"What on earth are you doing with a gun?" Eyes wide, Bowen released the clip, then checked the chamber for a stray round.

"I wanted something to protect myself with while you were gone." Lainey Jo thought it seemed logical—even smart.

Apparently, Bowen didn't share her opinion.

"So you decided to brandish a nine millimeter?"

"I wasn't *brandishing* anything. I was *holding* it."

"And where did you get it?" Bowen set the gun and the clip on the table, resting his hands on his hips and demanding an answer with the ice in his blue eyes.

"The woodstove."

"The woodstove?" he echoed.

"Yes. The woodstove." Lainey Jo pointed. "It was in there."

Bowen lifted his hand and dragged it across his forehead. When he lowered it, he also lowered his voice as if he were addressing a child. "This cabin belongs to another navy SEAL. If you snoop around, you'll probably find more weapons. Don't play with them. Leave them alone."

"So you'd rather I just get shot when you're not here?" Lainey challenged. She crossed her arms over her chest. This was ridiculous. He should be proud of her.

"Of course not. But do you know how to use a gun?"

"Yes." Lainey Jo quailed under his raised eyebrow. "Sort of."

Bowen drew in a slow breath. She had a feeling he was trying to manage his temper. When he let it back out, his countenance was more controlled. He was less patronizing and more respectful.

"Fair. I get you needed to feel safe."

"Thank you."

"But at least, let me teach you how to use it."

"That's fair." And it was. Lainey Jo wasn't going to pretend she was versed in the art of self-defense.

To lighten the mood, she pointed to the pencil on the table. "I thought of using that too."

Bowen lifted the pencil, and this time, a small smile cracked his mouth. "Huh. Not a bad idea. And it can't accidentally discharge or shoot someone's foot off."

Lainey Jo managed a wobbly smile. He was right. But so was she. She wasn't prepared to weaponize herself, but she also needed to know that she could take care of herself if it was called for.

Now, she bent and retrieved the pajamas Gramma Lou

had sent with Bowen. The sweatshirt was green with a quilted dog silhouette on the front. Beggars couldn't be choosers when it came to style, and for now, Lainey Jo was grateful to have something other than her dusty jeans and button-up blouse to sleep in.

With the weapons issue behind them for the moment, Bowen returned to unpacking the goods he'd brought along with him.

"There are cookies." Bowen rested a plastic container on the table. "And Gram also thought it best if you had a hot meal." He pulled out a thermos. "Beef stew. But I get some too."

His offhanded verification was enough to bring a smile to Lainey Jo's lips. She nodded. "That's only right."

"I thought so," he retorted.

"I can get some ready," she offered.

"I can get my own. You've had a big day."

She had. Lainey Jo didn't know what to say to his unexpected kindness, even if it was rough around the edges.

There was an uncomfortable silence between them.

The thermos with the stew sat on the table next to the gun.

"Quite the day," Lainey filled the silence with her empty words.

Bowen met her eyes. She looked into his. He had nice eyes when he wasn't being bossy.

He cleared his throat, and the moment was broken. "I'm going to go out and scout the perimeter. Go ahead and get supper if you want. You're probably hungry. I'll be back at nineteen-hundred."

Seven o'clock? That was thirty minutes from now.

"And——" Bowen hesitated.

She waited.

"Leave the gun alone. I don't want to get shot when I get back."

Lainey Jo nodded.

Bowen exited the cabin, and she locked the doors per his instruction. Her stomach growled. She hadn't eaten since breakfast, and now the idea of a chunky stew was about as close to perfect as she could get, considering the circumstances.

She made quick work of changing. Lainey Jo was tired of her jeans digging into her waist, and the idea of soft flannel pants sounded wonderful. With the buffalo plaid encasing her legs, she drew the sweatshirt over her head. There was no mirror, but Lainey Jo surveyed herself by looking at her reflection in a glass door on a small cabinet against the far wall.

"I look like a Christmas tree," she mumbled and immediately gave up hope of any sort of mutual attraction for her on Bowen's end. Not that she wanted him to be attracted to her. Not while she was running for her life and he was worried she was going to *brandish* a handgun like a cowboy from an old-fashioned Wild West show.

Her laugh caught in her throat and mingled with sudden tears. He hadn't meant to be unkind. She knew that. But his reaction had stung. His lack of faith in her ability to protect herself might be well-founded, but it made her feel less than capable. What would she do for the rest of her life? If she were in WITSEC, would there always be this lingering threat? Random shooters? Men chasing her in the alley? She thought the Witness Protection Program was just that. Protection. But here she was, hiding in a cabin with a stranger whose military background made him redeemable, but whose personality left her questioning.

Lainey Jo sniffed, looking around the room for a tissue.

The last thing she needed was to erupt into tears and have Bowen come back to find her a puddled mess on the floor. That would be two extremes. First gun-toting, then sobbing? He'd have every right to think she'd lost her mind.

But she could blame that on Uncle Chris. It was his fault she was here. His devious and pathetic nature had exploited others for the sake of his own gain.

For the next half hour, Lainey Jo worked on settling in. She didn't want to admit it, but she had to. Bowen's return to the cabin and being freed from the feeling she needed to have weapons for her self-defense brought a sense of calm to her that was both unexpected and welcome, and for the first time that day, Lainey Jo felt like she could think straight.

She found a set of clean, folded sheets in the cabinet with the glass door, along with a patchwork quilt and a pillowcase. Making the cot up, Lainey Jo could feel her body beginning to crave sleep.

But food. Food first.

She rummaged in the cupboards for bowls and, finding two mismatched glass ones, divvied up the stew. Spoons located, Lainey Jo reached for her bowl, eyeing the one she'd prepared for Bowen. Maybe she should have waited. If he took longer, it'd get cold being out of the thermos.

The coded rap on the door made her jump, and then Lainey Jo hurried to allow Bowen entry.

When she opened the door, his look of approval was reassuring. "Atta girl, Tadpole." He nodded. Then his attention was snagged by the stew, and he retrieved his bowl.

"Should we eat on the porch?" Lainey Jo suggested. Nothing sounded nicer to her than easing her body into one of the wooden porch chairs and listening to the creek sing as it bounced and rolled over rocks and boulders.

But Bowen's expression stopped her.

"Should we paint a bull's-eye on you, too?" he countered.

"Oh." Feeling scolded and not a little naive, Lainey Jo made her way to the cot and sank onto it, cupping her bowl in her lap.

Bowen stared at her for a long, silent moment. "Hey. I'm sorry. And I'm sorry for earlier, too. About the gun."

She lifted her eyes.

He continued. "I'm just trying to keep you safe. I wasn't trying to bite your head off."

"I know." She didn't, but it seemed like the right thing to say. Lainey Jo supposed, being in the military, Bowen wasn't trained to couch his words in empathy and indirect softness.

He leaned back against the table, using it as a way to rest as he spooned stew into his mouth. Chewing, he swallowed, and then cleared his throat. "Gram says I have the finesse of a grizzly bear."

Lainey Jo gave a small laugh. She could see that. Gramma Lou's observation made her like the woman even more. "Grizzly bears can be nice, though." She tried to offset his self-criticism.

His eyebrow winged upward. "Yeah, if you leave them alone."

"Should I leave *you* alone?" Lainey Jo asked before she could stop herself.

Bowen's spoon halted halfway to his mouth.

They stared at each other.

Suddenly, Lainey Jo wished she had just kept her mouth shut. Of course, he wished she would leave him alone. He could head into the mountains and hibernate like any self-respecting bear, and leave the prey to find their own way to survive.

She wasn't his problem, Lainey Jo acknowledged. She had no right to challenge anything Bowen Mays did or said on her behalf.

She had no right to challenge him. Not after dragging him into today's events. But he got it. She was shaken up, and now she was dealing with a rough-around-the-edges SEAL whose primary interaction with the emotions of a woman was when he was part of an extraction team. Tears were expected, and he was fine with that, but even then, it'd been Pax who'd been the sensitive one. Even the guys on the team gave Bowen space during tense situations. They knew he didn't sleep much. Knew he was tightly wound and intense. They also knew he just said things like they were.

Now he was staring at a wide-eyed, frightened woman who had regret painted across her face and was about ready to cry because it was obvious she realized she owed him and hadn't the right to get sassy with him. But, truth be told, he preferred sassy to histrionics. So…there *was* that.

"Nah." He finally managed an answer. "You don't have to leave me alone. I promise I won't bite."

"Just growl?" Lainey Jo managed to toss back with a wobbly smile.

Bowen graced her with a grin. Better to let her know she was safe to jest as long as she didn't cry. "Growling is a part of my DNA."

"Got it." Her eyes finally twinkled, and she ducked her head to look into her bowl of stew.

Bowen observed her for a moment, taking a few mouthfuls of Gramma Lou's beef amazingness. He'd circled the hunting shack, scoping out the places he felt were vantage points, and mentally mapping the area for when Pax arrived to help stand watch. But that'd be a few hours yet, Pax had told him when Bowen had called. He was in Sheridan, but he'd make it to the shack no later than twenty-three-hundred hours.

For now, Bowen wanted to assess the situation deeper by gathering more intel from Lainey Jo. He just hoped he could do so without upsetting her too much to the point she wasn't helpful.

"Tell me about your uncle," Bowen said.

Lainey Jo lifted her eyes.

Fine. So it was a command, not a request.

"Please," he tried adding.

Lainey seemed to consider for a moment and then nodded. "Have you heard of the Ludlow family?"

Bowen gave a short nod. "The rich family from out East?"

She nodded. Her eyes betrayed her.

Realization dawned. "Ohhhh," he dragged out the word. "Are you a Ludlow?"

Lainey Jo didn't have to respond. Everything about her was 100 percent readable.

"So you grew up with the Kennedys and those types of families?" Bowen asked, but she didn't need to bother answering. Anyone who was even slightly aware of American "royalty" knew the Ludlows were in the upper echelons of who's who. He wasn't entirely sure how the family had amassed their wealth, only that the Ludlow family had a few branches. Some were into politics, some into humanitarian aid, and others into business.

"Which Ludlow is your family branch?" he asked.

Lainey Jo set her now-empty bowl on the floor. "Scott Ludlow is my dad," she managed. "He runs a variety of organizations. His brother—my Uncle Chris—worked for him."

Bowen considered what he knew so far. "But your uncle had dealings in trafficking, and you turned witness on him?"

She nodded, but didn't expound.

"When was this?" he asked.

"Two years ago," Lainey Jo answered. "Actually, four. When I was twenty-two, it all started coming out. The FBI was running an investigation and, long story short, I'd been working with Uncle Chris as his assistant, and I stumbled on evidence that incriminated him."

"You were the primary witness?"

She nodded. Her face paled, and Lainey Jo wrapped her arms around herself as though she needed a hug and she was the only one who could give it to her. "It was a mess. Uncle Chris had threaded his entire ring through a lot of offshore accounts and under different company names. I won't even go into it all. But there were questions as to whether Dad was involved—which he wasn't. Everything checked out. Dad's financials, his investments, everything. But the FBI said that to make sure Dad wasn't implicated and that Uncle Chris was put away, I had to come forward with what I knew. They needed my testimony. Without me, there was no one else willing to talk against my uncle. So I gathered evidence for them, while I kept working for Uncle Chris. I gave it to the FBI, and that's how they took down Uncle Chris."

Bowen had to hand it to her. The woman had guts. Turning on any family member wasn't just hard, it was emotionally taxing, psychologically scarring, and as evidenced by today, physically dangerous. He'd missed the headlines of this story. Being overseas and focused on covert ops had him distanced from scandals back in the U.S. "How did your dad handle it? You turning witness on your uncle?"

Lainey Jo tipped her head back and forth. "He wasn't happy I was put in the situation I was by the FBI. He was *really* not happy that I entered WITSEC."

"I don't blame him," Bowen stated.

She looked at him.

"You're his daughter. His brother's crimes ruined your life."

Her eyes welled with unshed tears.

Great.

Bowen tried to be empathetic, and there were the waterworks. He scrambled to find something to say that wasn't as understanding, even as a small part of him felt like reaching out to hold her. Now that was an unexpected feeling!

"So they nailed your uncle?"

That worked.

Her tears dried, but she also grew ashen.

He needed to work on his delivery.

"The trial took forever. But he was sentenced, and he's been in prison for over a year now."

"And apparently, he has it out for you."

Lainey Jo sniffed, nodding, and making an obvious attempt to hold back tears. "I didn't expect him to go to these lengths, though. Not from behind bars."

Bowen shoved off the table and set his empty bowl down. "Your uncle must still have connections on the outside. Aside from revenge, what would be his motive? If your place was tossed, it sounds like he's looking for something."

She stared at him. Bowen thought he could almost see the wheels turning behind her eyes.

"I—" Lainey Jo shook her head slowly. "I don't know what he'd be looking for."

Bowen could tell she was perplexed. She wasn't hiding something from him. In a way, that was more worrisome.

If she had been, he could get it out of her and then have a clear mission. But if she didn't know why her uncle—assuming it *was* her uncle—was hunting her, that was dangerous on so many levels. It was difficult to devise a defense strategy, let alone an offense strategy.

"Was there anything at your uncle's trial that could have gotten him off the hook?" Bowen asked.

Lainey Jo leaned back on the cot, resting her shoulders against the wall. "I don't think so. The evidence was all there. I'd been able to gather files for the FBI. It was a solid case, they said."

"Did your uncle give you anything? Did anyone in your family give you anything? Something you might have brought with you into the program?"

Lainey Jo drew back, her expression grave. "No. I wasn't to have anything that tied me to my family. I left it all behind." She raised her hand and pushed her hair away from her face. It was apparent Lainey Jo was agitated by the way her hand trembled, but it didn't seem to be from the guilt of hiding something. More so, it appeared to be from the fear of the unknown.

"What do I do?" She almost whispered her question. "If you don't think it's safe to call the marshals…"

When she let her sentence hang, Bowen inserted his thoughts. "Not yet. With your handler dead, we need to know who we can trust. But before we can do that, you need to be safe." He hesitated, then pressed as gently as he could. "You're *sure* you don't know what someone might have been looking for in your apartment?"

"Am I sure?" Lainey Jo retorted with a watery laugh. "No. I think Uncle Chris—he probably hates me. If he found out where I live, then he wants me silenced."

"But why was your apartment ransacked?" Bowen

didn't want to interrogate Lainey Jo, but she did need to dig deep and consider that revenge might answer why someone wanted her dead, but it didn't resolve why they'd toss her place.

"I don't know why." Lainey Jo closed her eyes against his study of her face.

Bowen bit back a sigh and tried to summon what he'd seen Pax do when he was trying to come alongside a hurting woman but still gather information. He neared the cot and squatted in front of Lainey Jo.

She opened her eyes.

He captured them with as nice of a look as he could muster. Somehow, he needed to gain her complete trust, and to do that, Bowen knew he couldn't just bark orders.

"I think we need to go back to your place. You can collect a few things you might need, and then we'll sweep your apartment to see if there's anything that might trigger something in you. Something to tell us what your uncle is after—assuming it's your uncle who's behind all this."

Lainey Jo still held herself tense, but her eyes softened. "Is it safe?"

"It's not ideal," Bowen admitted. "But if we're smart about it, we can get in and out fast."

"My landlord is probably furious." Realization seemed to dawn on Lainey Jo, then. A shattered window. A torn-apart place.

Yeah. She wasn't wrong, but that was the least of their worries.

Bowen reached out and tapped her knee with his fingertips, withdrawing them almost the instant he tried to offer a comforting touch. "For now, we don't think about that. We stick together. We keep our heads on a swivel. We get in, we get out. We pray something triggers your recollection, and we can pinpoint what your uncle's target is."

"You mean, besides me?" she whispered, her gaze sinking so deeply into his, it was all Bowen could do not to reach out and pull her into the safety of his arms.

Taken off guard by the surge of unexpected feelings, Bowen pushed to his feet, looking down at her and trying to shield his face from exposing any emotion.

"Get some sleep," he grumbled. "We'll head out first thing in the morning. I'll be outside tonight." Bowen started for the door, hoisting his duffel bag over his shoulder. He paused. "Lock it behind me. Remember our knock. Stay away from the windows."

Lainey Jo looked like she was fighting between wanting to throw up, cry or collapse in exhaustion.

He tried to be comforting. "My buddy and I will keep watch. Get some sleep."

Shutting the door behind him, Bowen waited until he heard the bar lock shuttle into place. He had an hour yet before Pax would arrive. They could keep watch to the north on the ledge. The vantage point he scoped out was shielded yet provided a clear view of the cabin, both front and rear. They could dig in and wait the night out, and if necessary, Bowen was willing to show his enemy how a real sniper took a shot.

FIVE

Paxton Burke was nothing at all like Bowen. Lainey Jo shook the SEAL's hand, realizing she'd stereotyped all SEALs to be muscular and attractive simply because they were SEALs. She'd been right.

Pax's grin, however, was far less reserved than Bowen's, and his eyes practically sparkled with warmth and a side of humor. He clapped his hand on Bowen's shoulder as they sat down for coffee around the table in the hunting cabin.

"Big guy expected trouble. We both could've slept like babies if we'd wanted to." Pax took the mug of coffee Lainey Jo extended to him with a smile. He straddled a chair and drank with a noisy gulp.

"I'm just glad there was no trouble." Bowen also took his coffee, but he looked at it with an assessing eye before sipping it.

Lainey Jo wondered if there was anything Bowen did that wasn't analyzed and thought through first. Probably not. She shifted her attention to Pax, whose Latino features gave Bowen a run for his money in the looks department. But she noted that she hadn't relaxed until Bowen had come into the cabin behind Pax once they'd knocked and she'd unlocked the door. Nighttime had been restless, and while she was exhausted, it was difficult to fall into a state of complete trust.

A series of what-ifs raced through her mind all night.

What if the ones after her got to Bowen and Pax first?

What if Bowen and Pax couldn't stay awake?

What if Uncle Chris and his lackeys had figured out where she was hiding?

What if she were attacked while she slept?

There was nothing restful about those questions racing in her mind. So while she had faith that Bowen and Pax would do their unreserved best on her behalf, Lainey Jo had still slept with one eye open.

She'd made coffee this morning, figuring the men would come in needing some. As she looked at them now, she'd never know they hadn't slept a wink. She, on the other hand, probably looked not unlike a chicken who'd gone to war with a fox and barely made it out alive.

"That's good coffee," Pax affirmed.

"Good," Lainey Jo responded with a shaky smile, but her attention rested on Bowen who was standing to the side of one of the cabin windows. He had the curtain pushed back just enough to be able to see outside, while sipping the coffee he held in his right hand.

"We'll take off for your place in about fifteen minutes." He glanced at Lainey Jo, and she was very aware of her buffalo flannel pants and the green sweatshirt. "We'll finish our coffee outside so you can change out of your Christmas clothes."

He was teasing.

She could tell because there was a sudden glint in his eyes, and his left eyelid dropped in a wink.

Now that was uncalled-for behavior. Lainey Jo ducked

her head as she felt warmth creep up her face. Flirting was not part of the equation in keeping her safe.

For a brief second, it was hard to believe she'd known Bowen Mays for just under twenty-four hours, but her attention was snagged as Pax pushed his chair back from the table and hoisted his mug.

"Coffee refill and front porch it is." He refilled his coffee from the French press Lainey Jo had found in the cupboard, draining it before Bowen had a chance to top off his mug. He didn't seem to mind, though, Lainey Jo realized, because he was already headed out the door.

She noted the bulge of a gun tucked into the waistband of his cargo pants at the small of his back. Somehow, Lainey Jo had a feeling that wasn't the only weapon on him.

Once the men exited the cabin, Lainey Jo quickly changed into her clothes from yesterday. It would be nice to get a few things from her apartment, but her stomach was already in knots at the idea of it. She felt exposed and vulnerable at the idea of going back. There had to be a big possibility that whoever was chasing her would think to lay in wait for her there. But Bowen would have thought of that. Still, she had no idea how he intended to just walk through the front door, up the stairs and into her apartment without being seen.

As Lainey Jo finger-combed her hair, she realized trusting Bowen wasn't all that unlike trusting God. Of course, God was far more powerful and all-knowing, but the idea of trusting someone whose course of action you could not predict or understand was equally as unsettling.

Trust in the Lord. She memorized that Scripture verse as a child. The one from Proverbs, chapter three. Because her nanny had made a practice of reading her Bible stories before bed and instilling in Lainey Jo an element of faith she didn't get from her family.

She was thankful for that now. Even though God had a consistent habit of not telling her what He was doing with her life, He had always made a way for her. Lainey Jo glanced toward the door. As evidenced by the fact she had two navy SEALs drinking coffee on the porch and acting as her bodyguards when they owed her absolutely nothing.

In the next several minutes, Lainey Jo found herself sitting in the passenger seat of Bowen's truck. She was surprised when he handed her a baseball cap and a worn jean jacket.

"What's this for?"

"Put it on—" Bowen started, but Pax interrupted him from his place outside the truck, looking through the open driver's side window.

"*Please* put it on," he corrected Bowen with a laugh. "A little finesse, man." Pax shifted his attention to Lainey Jo, his eyes narrowing in a reassuring smile. "If you can tuck your hair back and put on the cap, plus put on Bowen's jacket, it'll make you look less like you. Looks like Bowen patched your head wound up with a nice butterfly bandage, so the hat shouldn't aggravate it too much."

Understanding, Lainey Jo returned Pax's smile. "Of course!" She gave him an exaggerated nod of her head and then dared to look at Bowen, whose scowl had deepened the furrow of his brows.

"Lighten up, Mr. Rogers." Pax patted the truck's door-frame and took a step back so Bowen could pull out. "Underneath that polite cardigan and pair of tennis shoes, we all know you're deadly."

A laugh followed them as Bowen pulled away.

"Mr. Rogers?" Lainey Jo queried, not able to help herself as she carefully positioned the hat so it didn't rub on her head wound. It was still sore, but the original throbbing and mind-numbing pain had passed.

"The team calls me that. 'Cause I'm so *nice*." The irony in Bowen's voice was thick. There was also a strange edge to it that made Lainey Jo give him a second glance. For a moment, she wondered if Bowen actually *wanted* to be more Mr. Rogers-nice than he was. As if he tried, but just didn't quite know how.

"I see." Lainey Jo felt an overwhelming need to reassure the exceptionally capable soldier. "Well," she added for Bowen's sake, "I've never really been that fond of cardigans on men, myself." She shrugged into his jean jacket, engulfed with the scents that settled into its denim. Scents associated with a man. Grease. Pine. Fresh air.

Lainey Jo was rewarded with a soft chuckle.

"Oh yeah?"

Bowen's sideways glance did something to Lainey Jo's stomach that was most assuredly unsettling, but not in a fearful sort of way.

She quickly directed her attention to the visor as she caught a glimpse of her reflection. "Yeah," she replied.

Lainey Jo knew she had to get her wits about her. Now wasn't the time to get all smitten by a man with arms as hard as stone, and a chiseled jaw that could probably sharpen a knife.

Her apartment door opened with Bowen's lock-picking expertise. Lainey Jo didn't have her keys because of her frantic escape yesterday, and her well-meaning neighbor must have called the landlord because her apartment had been locked.

Bowen had driven in a bewildering pattern of unnecessary turns and side roads to get there. She knew he was trying to make sure no one followed them and no one spotted them. They'd kept an easy but steady gait to the complex's entrance, Bowen's arm wrapped around her waist. He'd pulled her to his side as they walked, and even though he'd tipped his head toward her ear as if he were romantically engaged with her, she could almost feel his eyes burning track marks across the top of her head as he surveyed the area.

Now, Bowen pushed into her apartment first, gun drawn as a precautionary measure. Once she stepped in, Bowen motioned for her to shut and lock the door.

He held his hand out in a gesture to keep her behind him and communicate that she should stay by the door. In a few strides, he'd made it to the living room window that spanned a good portion of the wall. There was a shattered hole in the glass where the bullet had penetrated yesterday, and Lainey Jo could hear the wind whistling through. She was sure her landlord had probably been speed-dialing her—perhaps even called the cops.

Bowen ignored the damaged window, dropping the blinds with one hand while alert with his firearm in the other. He twisted the rod so the blinds closed. With a sharp look that communicated she needed to stay where she was, he disappeared down the short hall, clearing the closet, the bathroom and then the bedroom. She heard more blinds shutting in the bedroom, and then he stepped out.

"Okay." He repositioned his gun in the waistband of his pants. "We're good for now, but let's be quick."

Lainey Jo moved forward at Bowen's nod, and she hurried into her bedroom, stepping over the mess that was still strewn about the place. Pillows slashed with stuffing coming out of them, a chair overturned, and in her bedroom, she saw whoever had ransacked the place had pulled out her dresser drawers, flinging her clothes every which way.

She tugged a backpack from the closet and made quick work of throwing some items inside. A pair of jeans, a few T-shirts, underwear and socks, and her favorite pink sweat-shirt that she'd bought when she'd first arrived in Wyoming. It had a buffalo on its front and the words "look, don't pet" in black lettering over it. Gathering toiletries, she was very aware Bowen was pacing in the front room.

"Five more minutes," he called out without raising his voice.

"Okay." She wasn't about to argue. Every nerve in her body was on high alert, and being here—being home—felt horribly unsafe.

"Take a look around you." Bowen caught her attention as she crossed the hall back to her bedroom. She paused and he issued her a look that took her back to the previous night's conversation. "See if you can pinpoint anything—or if anything triggers something that might give you an idea of what your uncle is after."

Lainey Jo nodded but knew it was pointless. She didn't have anything Uncle Chris would still want. Besides, so what if she did? He'd already been convicted and sentenced. Even if she *had* something, it wouldn't make any differ-ence now.

At least, that's what she told herself as she swept her gaze around her bedroom. Everything in the room felt cold and impersonal to her. There were no childhood memories, no souvenirs from high school, no photographs of her par-ents. It was, instead, a few paintings of Parisian walkways, a silk potted fern in the corner, a comforter in shades of gray and peach, and a bookshelf with a few books and a ceramic statue of a cat.

"There's nothing here." She lifted her eyes to Bowen, who stood in the doorway.

"Move into the bathroom then." He stepped aside so she could pass, and Lainey Jo stifled a sigh. She wouldn't have hidden anything in the bathroom, and if she had, she would have remembered it.

But the man was unwavering in his orders, and she didn't have the energy to argue. Lainey Jo did her due diligence and meandered through the tiny bathroom. Shower, check. Bathroom cupboard, check. Toilet paper, a basket of toiletries on the counter, and the medicine cabinet.

"Nothing." She addressed Bowen.

He nodded and said, "Kitchen?"

This time, Lainey Jo didn't try to hide her annoyance. She pressed her lips together and dropped her shoulders in the weight of exasperation as she pushed past him.

"I would know if I'd hidden something."

Her resistance was met with silence.

Lainey Jo scanned the kitchen. Tiny table, sink, no dishwasher, medium-sized fridge, a few bags of chips on the counter, hot pad, a toaster, cookie jar, coffee mug rack and a spray bottle of kitchen cleaner.

"The salt and pepper shaker." Lainey Jo pointed to the plain white ones that sat by the cookie jar.

Bowen surged toward them, and Lainey Jo couldn't help but laugh aloud.

"I'm kidding!" She waved off the inane objects.

The man leveled an icy glare at her. "This isn't a game, Lainey Jo."

No. No, it wasn't. And they were wasting time. "I know. But I don't *have* anything," Lainey Jo insisted.

"Whoever tossed the place was looking for something." Bowen's retort awakened some of Lainey Jo's internal fight.

"Probably looking for me!" she shot back.

"In a pillow?" Bowen waved his hand toward one of the sliced throw pillows on the couch that had stuffing busting out of its innards.

Lainey Jo considered. His point wasn't misdirected. She had no explanation for the pillow. The salt and pepper shakers had been meant to be her attempt to lighten the mood. But now, she glanced at them, and they seemed to mock her from their position at the base of the cookie jar.

A cold hand of panic gripped her.

The cookie jar.

Lainey Jo stared at it, the blue jar alone and empty on the counter. It was a fixture. It had been there since she moved in. She didn't bake. She never filled it with cookies. She even forgot it was there on the counter.

"What is it?" Bowen looked between her and the counter in an obvious attempt to identify what had snagged Lainey Jo's attention.

She eyed the jar. "I—the cookie jar."

It came back to her then. The day she moved into the apartment. The shock of all the events that transpired making her movements almost robotic. She'd unpacked her scarce belongings. Some new clothes. Shoes. Things for the bathroom.

Then she'd pulled a stuffed toy cat from where she'd tucked it in the toe of a tennis shoe she had packed. It wasn't a large animal. She could hold it with one hand, and it squished down small.

Contraband.

Lainey Jo remembered now. She had excused her behavior by thinking everyone who went into the Witness Protection Program had to have at least one thing of home that they snuck in. And no one would give the slightest care about a pink-furred, stuffed animal.

Uncle Chris had given it to her when she was little.

After the awfulness of all that had transpired, Lainey Jo wanted nothing else than to return to the days when she was eight. When Uncle Chris was her handsome, big hero. When he gave her the cat and promised he'd always be her "furever uncle."

Now she had betrayed him.

For a moment, it didn't matter the atrocities Uncle Chris had committed. What mattered was that he was her Uncle Chris. The man who'd taught her to swim in her parents' pool, the man who'd played hours of Checkers with her when she was in middle school, and the man who convinced her parents to let her work for him instead of pursuing a Master's degree. She'd been done with education. Her parents wanted more from her. Uncle Chris had seen Lainey Jo's desire to get on with life.

Now, it all came back to her.

She'd sequestered the cat in the cookie jar in order to keep it out of sight. Her one link to home. Her smuggled souvenir. The one she'd forgotten since she'd arrived, and her grief over the broken relationship turned to denial and then bitterness.

Bitterness had made her forget the cat.

As she stared at the jar, Bowen followed her line of sight. In two long strides, he was at the jar and yanked the lid off. It clanked as he set it on the counter and reached inside. Pulling out the well-loved pink cat, he held it toward her.

"What's this?"

There was an accusation in his voice.

"I—" Lainey Jo's throat clogged with guilt and tears. "It's just a cat."

"There's no such thing as 'just a cat' when your place has been trashed." Bowen began to massage the animal, but was distracted as he glanced at his watch. "We're out of time. Let's go."

He started for the door, then turned. Lainey Jo noticed he tried to temper his expression and gentle his words. "Please. Come. We'll talk about this in the truck and figure it out. But for now, we need to move."

Lainey Jo slung her backpack over her shoulder, sheepish and guilt-ridden for not thinking about the cat. But it was just a stuffed toy. It was nothing.

No man of Uncle Chris's caliber would send someone to loot her apartment to look for a sentimental toy he had probably long forgotten existed.

But then again, Lainey Jo had thought she'd known Uncle Chris.

It was obvious now, she hadn't. Not at all.

It was the epitome of rude to say "I told you so," so he didn't, but everything in Bowen's gut had been accurate. He could tell Lainey Jo had forgotten about the stuffed cat and whatever it meant to her. Trauma had a way of allowing individuals to block certain things from their memories. Whether it was of a specific event, or elements that contributed to a situation as a whole. He didn't blame Lainey Jo, and he didn't believe she'd hidden the stuffed toy from him on purpose.

Two questions nagged at him, though. The first question was why the person who'd torn Lainey Jo's apartment apart hadn't checked a very obvious cookie jar on the counter. Then, was it the toy that they'd been after? It was, after all, a toy.

Bowen had every intention of taking the animal apart

and seeing what it might be harboring, but now wasn't the time. It wasn't the time to ask the questions either. Instead, he needed to get Lainey Jo back to the truck and then weave his way back to the safe house.

Compliant, Lainey Jo followed him through the hall of the apartment building. She had every right to question how he knew his way around, and if she asked later, he'd explain that he accessed blueprints for the building and had done his own surveillance before ever bringing her here.

Now, he pushed open the heavy metal door to the back staircase. The apartment building seemed all but deserted, with it being midday and all. He assumed most of its inhabitants were away at work, so there was an element of subtlety allowed them as they slipped down the back staircase.

Lainey Jo's face was white. Bowen could only imagine she was recalling her flight from the building after she'd been shot at. He was praying for a less dramatic exit this time.

Within minutes, they'd exited the building and made their way at a brisk pace back to the public lot where Zeke sat with its rusted fenders, waiting for them.

"Get in," Bowen commanded.

Lainey Jo was quick to listen, and once Bowen had climbed into the driver's seat, he fired up the engine.

"Keep your head down," he stated as he put the truck into reverse.

"Do you see someone? Are we being followed?" There was panic in her voice. She hunched over in the seat.

Bowen used his mirrors to back the truck out of its spot and he quickly shifted into Drive and pressed the gas. "Not that I see, but I always act as if we are."

"I didn't remember the cat." Lainey Jo's voice was watery with guilty admission as Bowen pulled the truck from the lot and onto the main street.

So far, so good.

"I—it was a gift from my Uncle Chris."

Any confidence or argumentativeness that spoke to Lainey Jo's spunk had dissipated. Bowen had to admit, he missed it. He had seen a glimpse of who Lainey Jo might have been if her life hadn't taken such a twist. But instead, she was beaten down, afraid and on the run.

In a way, he understood how she felt. It was agonizing not to be the person you knew God had intended you to be. But at least in Lainey Jo's situation, she was a victim. In his? He was just a straight-up failure.

Bowen spotted the car three vehicles behind him. It had turned onto the road not long after they'd left the parking lot. He took a quick right at the next street. Sure enough, after a few moments, the car also turned right. It hung back and put no pressure on him.

"We've got a tail," Bowen said aloud.

"What!" Lainey Jo's reaction wasn't one of surprise. He'd made it very clear it was a risk they'd taken to even come here. Her response was one of fear. She might as well have asked him what they were going to do.

He decided to answer her unspoken question. "I'm going to try to shake it. I don't think they picked us up at the apartment. I'm not sure how they tracked us, but they did."

Lainey Jo, still bent at the waist, her head held close to her knees, looked up at him. "Did they put a GPS tracker on your truck?"

He hid a smile. She was either smart, or she'd watched too much TV.

"Anything's possible. But I doubt it. There wouldn't have

been any opportunity for them to do that, and they would've most likely ambushed us at the apartment."

"So they were just waiting for us to show up?"

"It's what I would've done." Bowen checked the rear mirror. Yep. Still there.

"And we still went?"

He didn't blame Lainey Jo for the disbelief in her tone.

"I didn't think we had much choice. We need to get out ahead of your uncle or whoever is behind all of this."

"Let me just call the marshals—"

"No." Bowen regretted his bark, but he had just turned left on a meaningless road, and it was a for sure thing they were being followed.

"But why not?"

There it was. Some of the feistiness was returning to her voice.

"I told you. Your contact in the marshals was killed between the time we arranged to meet up and then arrived. We don't know who you can trust."

"Or maybe they'd bugged Marshal Halloway's phone?" Lainey Jo suggested.

Bowen had to admit, the thought had crossed his mind. What he despised right now was the lack of intel. There were too many variables to come up with a firm plan of action yet. And now? They knew to associate his truck with Lainey Jo.

"Great." Bowen scowled.

"What?"

He shot Lainey Jo a glance as his mind moved several plays ahead, figuring how to shake their tail. Once they did, it was only a matter of time before they tracked Zeke to Gramma Lou's place and to him. The safe house was likely still secure, but Gramma Lou was not.

Lainey Jo was still watching him, waiting for an answer. He didn't have time to elaborate, but he also didn't regret the harsh truth behind his answer. Lainey Jo deserved to know.

"They know who I am now. Which means—"

"Gramma Lou!" Lainey Jo's intake of breath affirmed Bowen's assessment that she was sharp enough to put pieces together.

"Hang on," Bowen said. "We're going to get rid of this guy, and then we need to get to Gramma Lou. And fast."

SIX

Lainey Jo paced the inside of the cabin. Bowen had evaded whoever had been tailing them. Every nerve in her body was tight, wanting Bowen to drive straight to Gramma Lou's and get her. But Bowen had been right not to. They would lead their tracker directly to her if they had, and this way, the ridiculous route they took back to the safe house confirmed, after a decent amount of time, that they had truly gotten rid of them. After a careful journey back to the safe house, Bowen had left her there with instructions to stay put, stay low and stay inside.

Pax had met them there, and the men swapped vehicles. Bowen, in Pax's black truck, took off to retrieve Gramma Lou.

"I'll be around," Pax assured her, and then left her to stand watch.

This was all her fault. All of it. Lainey Jo dropped onto the cot and buried her face in her hands. Bowen hadn't asked to be pulled into her drama, and for certain, neither had Pax or Gramma Lou. It was unfair to expect them to guard her, and it was horrific to even imagine anyone going after Gramma Lou to get to her.

Lainey Jo raked her fingers through her hair. She caught sight of the pink fur of the cat sticking out of the zipper on her backpack. Jumping to her feet, Lainey Jo went to retrieve it.

A cat? A stuffed cat?

It made no sense that anyone would destroy her apartment to find a stuffed cat that was in a cookie jar in plain sight and then leave it behind!

Lainey Jo looked at the glass eyes with purple irises. She remembered the day Uncle Chris had given her this cat. She'd been eight—maybe ten. It didn't matter. Lainey Jo shook her head trying to remember the details in case something about them answered the questions of today.

"There's my little pipsqueak."

Lainey Jo recalled how Uncle Chris had rounded the family's in-ground pool, dressed to the nines in a tuxedo with a white bow tie. She'd always thought he was handsome. Clark Kent handsome, but her young self was also sure he could fly too. He would if she asked him to.

Uncle Chris had crouched down beside her. She wasn't swimming. The pool was off limits without her parents around, and Lainey Jo had always been an obedient kid. Her father, while not overtly affectionate, was free to dole out his pride in her when she obeyed. So that's what she did. It felt good for her father to be proud of her.

But when it wasn't her father, it was Uncle Chris. And that night, he'd seen the sadness in her eyes.

"What's wrong, pipsqueak?" he'd asked.

"Daddy told me he wants me to go to summer school."

"Ahhhhh, that. Yes, I did hear something about that."

"But it's a boarding *school!"* Lainey Jo remembered the utter terror she had felt when her father told her she was not just going to a boarding school over the summer, but she was going to a boarding school in France.

"France is a beautiful place." Uncle Chris had tried to make her feel better.

"I don't like shallots and I don't like snails." Lainey Jo was sure that was all French people ate.

And then, in typical Uncle Chris style, he had reached into the pocket of his tuxedo jacket and pulled out the stuffed, pink cat.

"What if you take this little guy with you. He told me he needed some love."

That was it. The cat became her sidekick for the entire summer in France. She'd learned to like shallots, if not snails, and when she'd come home, a newly matured nine-year-old—or so she'd thought—she'd placed the cat on her dresser. She didn't need to sleep with him anymore. She was home.

But the pink cat had always been there. Ever since. And when she'd left, he had to come with her. ·

"What do I do? What do I do?" Panic lodged in her gut. She knew what Bowen had told her to do.

Stay put, stay low.

But that didn't help anyone.

Her options were limited. She could do as Bowen asked. The pros of that choice would be to have two SEALs managing the situation. She couldn't get much better than that. But it still left Gramma Lou inextricably linked to the danger. That was unacceptable as far as Lainey Jo was concerned.

Option number two would be to pursue her original idea to get in contact with the US Marshals. By now, they *had* to be looking for her, didn't they? What if they were the ones tailing Bowen, and for good reason, with good intent? Bowen seemed reticent to trust them. He had made a good argument for that position. But so had she. She knew

Uncle Chris had plenty of resources and could have gotten a trace on Marshal Halloway's calls. Maybe that was what had tipped off Uncle Chris's people?

Of course, she was speculating, but wasn't Bowen?

The cons of option number two were pretty obvious to Lainey Jo. She would be putting herself out there, by herself, in the thick of danger. There were at least two men after her—which was no comfort—and without Bowen, she knew she'd run a high risk of being seen. Not to mention, if she were to try to get somewhere and purchase a burner phone, she'd need transportation.

Lainey Jo looked at the door as if she could see through it. The only option there was to steal the truck Bowen affectionately called "Zeke."

But if she could call the number the marshals had given her for situations like this, then they could intervene and it would release Gramma Lou from the threat of danger. Bowen and Pax, too.

Lainey Jo pushed to her feet.

What choice did she have? It was selfish to expect three almost-strangers to put themselves in the line of fire just to protect her. It wasn't their fault that her uncle was devious and wicked and obviously still well connected to the outside world, even from prison.

Worst case, she could call her father, couldn't she? Part of the reason Dad had been upset that she'd joined WIT-SEC was that he was convinced he could buy her enough protection for her to keep her existing lifestyle. He probably could have. But that was also risky, because it kept her close to the family and—

Lainey Jo released a pent-up growl. She could go around in circles with the what-ifs, the should-haves, and the todos. The fact was, she just needed to pick the option she felt was the wisest.

For her own personal safety? That was to listen to exactly what Bowen said.

For everyone else's safety?

Lainey Jo snatched a sweatshirt from the back of the chair, and the motion caused the chair to topple to the cabin floor with a bang. She ignored it and yanked the cabin door open.

She paused in the doorway.

Pax wasn't in view—but that wasn't a surprise. He was probably hunkered down somewhere keeping tabs on the cabin, or else he was circling their perimeter to verify their security.

But there it was. Zeke, Bowen had called it. The silver, rusty truck. Lainey Jo had seen Bowen toss the keys onto the dash. It made sense. If they needed to get away fast, no one wanted to try to remember who had the keys or where they were. There was no risk out here of the truck being stolen.

Lainey Jo bit back an inopportune smile.

Or so Bowen Mays believed.

"That was too easy," Lainey Jo stated as she bounced in Zeke's cab. She found her way to the main road through trial and error. Bowen had taken so many twists and turns to get her to the safe house that it was astonishing that Lainey Jo was able to find pavement. The vehicle lurched as the terrain shifted from dirt to asphalt. Lainey Jo couldn't help but feel a bit of relief at being on a normal road. She would be able to find her way now.

She adjusted the brim of her baseball cap. It probably did little good. She was in a marked vehicle as far as the men chasing her were concerned. Wearing a baseball cap wasn't going to hide her identity and fool them in the slightest.

Lainey Jo could only pray now. Her decision had been made, and she was driving into the thick of it. Bowen would be furious, but long-term, she owed him nothing. There was no relationship outside of the last forty-eight hours, and while she could argue that she owed him a great deal for all he'd done, breaking ties was only going to be payment for it.

It stung, though. She wasn't going to lie to herself. The last segment of time had been terrifying, but it had also reintroduced Lainey Jo to how it felt not to be alone. Not to go solo.

"I prefer it," she declared.

Fine. She was talking to a truck. But she was sans friends at the moment, or human companionship. She didn't even have a dog! So a truck was it, and the nice thing was, Zeke wasn't going to argue back.

"I prefer not being alone," Lainey Jo restated, just in case Zeke hadn't comprehended her observation. His spark plugs may be clogged or malfunctioning, which could affect his hearing.

She was losing her mind!

Lainey Jo sucked in a stabilizing breath and prayed the oxygen to her brain would clear up her senses enough to bring her back into reality.

She caught a glimpse of the green road sign that flew past. It was twelve miles to town. Once there, Lainey Jo knew exactly where she could go to get a phone. Cash was in her pocket. She was debating whether it was wiser to head out of town once she got the phone and try to make it to a safer, secluded area, or if it was better to stay where there was population. But then, the population hadn't seemed to stop the would-be sniper from trying to kill her in broad daylight, and she certainly didn't want to put anyone at risk.

"They'll tell me what to do," Lainey Jo reassured herself—and Zeke—of the US Marshals' know-how. She just needed to make a connection with them.

Soon, the tiny store on the outskirts of town came into view. Lainey Jo pulled into a parking spot and shut off the engine.

"Stay put and stay down," she muttered to Zeke as she pocketed its key. Of course, the truck wasn't going anywhere, but she was, and all she kept hearing in her mind was Bowen's instructions on repeat.

Lainey Jo could only imagine the look on his face when he found out what she'd done. But then, she'd never really know what his reaction would be, because she'd never see him again.

A bell chimed as she pushed open the door to the store. It was a store that sold a little of everything, and Lainey Jo was met with a blast of cool air—someone was still working the A/C even though it was fall—and a mixture of smells. Pine pellets for horse bedding, grease for machinery and a perfumy whiff of air freshener.

The linoleum floor was scuffed beneath her feet. Lainey Jo paused on one of its squares and directed her attention to the narrow orange signs that hung over the aisles. She just needed electronics. A prepaid cell phone. Nothing more.

One of those large round mirrors hung from the ceiling, giving a view of the entrance behind her. A woman and two kids were on their way in, and Lainey Jo released a relieved breath. So far, so good.

"Can I help you?"

Lainey Jo squawked at the attendant's polite inquiry and

jumped back, jarring her shoulder against a spinning rack of birthday card options.

"I'm so sorry," the young woman laughed sheepishly. "I didn't mean to scare you."

"No. I—uh—" Lainey Jo brushed off the apology. The woman's nametag read "Eva," and she had a pleasant, round face with freckles and wore an orange vest with the store's logo embroidered in purple just over her heart. "Do you have any prepaid phones?" Lainey Jo managed. She glanced at the overhead mirror.

Still safe.

Eva's eyebrows rose, and she nodded with more excitement than Lainey Jo felt was due a prepaid phone. "For sure! They're right over here."

Lainey Jo would never have found the phones. They were tucked into a small section between dog leashes and facial tissues. After she gave Eva a quick nod of thanks, the woman moved away, and Lainey Jo made fast work of picking out a phone. There were only two choices, and she expected to make just one call, assuming everything went as planned.

She heard the chime of the door opening and stilled.

Taking an instinctive step closer to the shelf, Lainey Jo tilted her head so she could look at the mirror. It was out of her viewpoint. Voices murmured at the front counter. Lainey Jo couldn't tell if they were male or female, but her senses were on high alert.

She eased her way to the end of the aisle, carefully looking out and around it.

"Whatcha buyin'?"

Lainey Jo bit back a yelp.

A little girl stood in front of her, purple sticky lips, a lollipop in one hand, and huge brown eyes staring up at her.

Lainey Jo managed a wobbly smile just as the girl's mother appeared from the next aisle over.

"I'm so sorry!" She corralled her daughter and scooted off in the opposite direction.

Lainey Jo took the opportunity to trail behind her, finally able to catch a clear view of the front checkout counter.

It was an older man leaning on a cane, with a woman who appeared to be of similar age next to him. They were paying for their items.

Which meant, whoever had entered the store had already disappeared somewhere inside of it.

"I need to get out of here," Lainey Jo muttered to herself. Get the phone, get out, get to Zeke. That was her mission.

And stay alive.

That was also a critical part.

She made her way to the counter and Eva was there, her perky smile oblivious to the alarm bells ringing in Lainey Jo.

"Will that be all?"

Lainey Jo wondered why cashiers were trained to ask that. If she needed more items, why would she be in line to pay for what she had? Biting back snark she knew was because of the tension mounting in her, Lainey Jo just nodded. She scanned the store.

"*Keep your head on a swivel.*" Lainey Jo could hear Bowen in her mind instructing her to be aware.

She caught sight of a man at the far back of the store but down the aisle directly in line with the register. His back was to her, but the way he held his body reminded her of someone who wasn't shopping, but was looking for something—or someone.

If they had already found her, she was in trouble!

"Miss?"

Lainey Jo returned her attention to Eva. "I'm sorry, what?"

Eva repeated the total, and Lainey Jo dug into her pocket for her cash. She handed Eva the money, and Eva prattled on about the weather as she made change.

"Thanks." Lainey Jo took the offered money and stuffed it into the pocket of her jeans.

She glanced back at the man.

He'd disappeared.

"Do you want a bag for that?" Eva asked.

"No," Lainey Jo snapped. "Thank you," she added, attempting to soften her response. But she didn't even bother to look at Eva. Instead, she reached for the phone housed in its packaging and tucked her head in as she made for the front door.

She glanced up at the mirror before she exited.

Lainey Jo froze.

He was looking at her from just down the aisle.

Her eyes met the stranger's and the instant they did, Lainey Jo knew she'd been found.

"No, no, no!" Lainey Jo sprinted from the store, clutching the phone in her hand. There was no time to open it, to activate it, let alone make a call.

Did she dare race back to Zeke? Try to make a getaway? It seemed the smartest, so Lainey Jo ran toward the truck only to skid to a slowed halt when she saw a man on the other side of Zeke—on the driver's side and just out of recognizable view of her.

"Help me!" Her desperate prayer was uttered as she diverted to the left and side of the store toward the alleyway.

She could hear footsteps behind her, slamming onto the surface.

"Hey!" someone shouted.

There was a collision. The sound of a garbage can being knocked over and a shopping cart wheeling metallically as something crashed into it.

"Watch where you're going!" Another shout. It was directed at whoever was chasing her, but Lainey Jo didn't take a second to look back.

She dodged a dumpster, debating on trying to hide behind it. But she could hear her assailant closing in and knew it was fruitless. He would see her.

Lainey Jo swiped at a random stack of empty, plastic milk crates sitting behind the building. Her action sent them catapulting across the asphalt. A brief deterrent but it might buy her a second or more.

She frantically scanned ahead of her. The alley had a few cars parked perpendicular to the buildings. There was a dumpster, it seemed, by every back door. The main highway was in view at the end of the alley. If she could make it there, she could—she could—she didn't know what she could do! She hadn't anticipated running on foot.

At any moment, the odds were high a bullet would slam into her back. Lainey Jo could almost hear it. The gun discharging. The man chasing her watching as his bullet met its mark, sending her sprawling to the ground.

But there was no gunshot.

Only the persistent sound of running footsteps and a grunt as the man hurdled a wayward milk crate.

Lainey Jo increased her speed, but she'd never been a fast runner. She'd never been truly athletic, if she were honest. She veered around wooden pallets leaning against the side of a building.

She was going to make it!

Once she hit the main highway, Lainey Jo hoped she

could dodge traffic and get to the other side. It was only a four-lane highway, and on the other side, she knew there was a deep culvert and then a park. She could find a place to hide and hopefully buy herself enough time to call the marshals. Maybe she'd even run into an on-duty cop or something.

She could do it. She could make it. She—

Lainey Jo slammed into the ground, the filthy asphalt of the alleyway rising up to meet her as two arms wrapped around her legs, tackling her. The phone, in its plastic packaging, went flying from her grip. Lainey Jo's hands scraped along the ground and she could feel the abrasions from the stones and grit of the alley.

She twisted, trying to free herself from the man.

"Let me go!" Lainey Jo yelled. She kicked at the man's face, but he was too strong.

"Knock it off!" His fist slammed into her shoulder, and he shoved her onto her back.

Lainey Jo's head hit the ground. Pain sliced through her, her head throbbing even as her shoulder screamed against her attacker's violence.

"Where is it?" He pressed his forearm just below her throat, straddling her and holding her down with his weight.

"Where is what?" she managed to choke out. But she knew. She knew what he wanted. She just didn't know why.

"Where is the toy cat?"

He wasn't even going to be cryptic. Lainey Jo looked into his face, the weathered creases in his cheeks, and around his eyes. Narrow eyes, and green, with thick eyebrows of a chestnut shade. His hair was tucked under a baseball cap not unlike her own.

Her cap. Where was her cap? For a brief, surreal moment, it was all Lainey Jo could focus on. She didn't remember the baseball cap Bowen had given to her falling off her head. But it must have. It must have been lost somewhere between the store and her flight down the alley.

"I said, where is the cat?" Her assailant's insistent shove brought Lainey Jo back to the present.

Her foggy, pain-filled mind cleared for a moment.

"What do you want it for?" she managed.

"Doesn't matter." He spit out the words, pressing his face close to hers. "Give me the toy or it's over."

"It's already over," she retorted. Lainey Jo might not be versed in the skill of escape or evasion, but she was able to recognize reality when it stared her in the face.

There was no way this man was going to let her go. She could tell him where the stuffed cat was, and once he found it, she'd be dead. But there was no way she was going to tell him the cat was in Zeke, tucked away in her duffel bag. She may not know why Uncle Chris wanted it so badly, but if it was this critical, then it boded no good for anyone.

SEVEN

She brought her knee up hard. It was instinctual, and Lainey Jo didn't restrain the amount of force she put into it.

Her attacker grunted as he stiffened, but he didn't release the pressure against her as he pinned her to the ground.

"You little—"

She cut off his words as she managed to kick up once more, her body bucking under the assailant's. It was enough for him to lose his hold on her, and Lainey Jo took the chance to bring her hands up to his face and, in a split second, she jammed her thumbs against his eyes.

The man yelled, rolling off of her, but Lainey Jo rolled with him. She delivered another well-aimed kick with her foot, and the man crumpled into the fetal position. His eyes were squeezed shut against the pain of her forceful attack.

Lainey Jo wasted no time. Even as her head and body throbbed from the attack, she ran from the alley, desperation more heightened than the need to recover.

The funny thing was, it was Uncle Chris who had taught her the self-defense move she'd used on the man. It wasn't well executed, but she'd managed.

"They say go for a man's groin, but if you can, go for their eyes. Once you blind them, they're useless."

As she made it to the end of the alley, the man still

groaning on the ground behind her, Lainey Jo wasn't sure she'd applied enough pressure to literally blind him. But she certainly wasn't going to remain to find out.

It wasn't lost on her that in the very close past, where there was one man hunting her, there was another. This must be the one who didn't mind up close and personal, which meant the supposed sniper was still out there. He might have been the man she'd seen standing by Zeke. She was sure the guy she'd left rolling on the ground behind her was the man who'd been in the store. Still, Lainey Jo knew there was another culprit.

She didn't know enough to know if he'd have a gun trained on her or not. Was there anywhere to set up a rifle? Had he had time? Lainey Jo regretted ever leaving the safe house, because now she was once again without a way to contact the Marshals and, in this day and age, pay phones weren't on every street corner like her mom had told her they used to be.

The highway was busier than she'd expected. Lainey Jo hesitated on the shoulder. There were rows of buildings and stores in this direction. She could potentially run into any of them and ask someone to call the police. But she wasn't sure how long the guy behind her would stay down, and if he regained his vision, Lainey Jo had no doubt sheer fury would send him after her now. Stuffed cat or not.

It seemed better to cross the highway and get to the park, which had been her original quick plan. But was it? She had no idea. Lainey Jo knew she had no time to spare deciding. The idea of running into a nearby building was comforting, but she had a feeling that comfort was deceptive. He'd find her, and——Lainey Jo looked over her shoulder and down the alley——he was already stumbling to his feet!

She assessed the traffic and made a fast dash in a clear

spot to the median strip between the lanes that went east and west. A truck honked its horn as it passed her.

Yes, yes! She knew this was a no crossing zone! But the truck had already whizzed past along with a myriad of others. Lainey Jo could see a gap in traffic coming up, and she waited. A red car flew by and then a green one and then, after a silver minivan, Lainey Jo took off across the next set of two lanes.

She heard a shout behind her above the roar of the traffic. Whether it was the guy who'd attacked her or another driver, she had no idea.

Once Lainey Jo's feet landed on the gravel shoulder, she made quick work of stumbling down the side of the embankment by the culvert. The park lay ahead of her. A green lawn of mowed grass, beautiful maple trees and park benches welcomed her. There was a small fountain in the middle of the park, and to the west, Lainey Jo saw a playground. She would *not* lead anyone in the direction of where children may be.

East it was.

Lainey Jo dashed to her left, thankful to see a sidewalk that wove around into a grove of decorative trees and shrubs. It gave her cover for a moment. She rounded the curving corner of the walkway and dove beneath the branches of a dogwood tree, rolling under a line of evergreen shrubbery behind it. The branches poked through her shirt, but Lainey Jo squeezed beneath them, hoping the thickness of the shrubs would offer hiding space.

The park had been curiously empty of people. Maybe because it was late in the afternoon. School was getting out. People weren't taking afternoon strolls but heading home to make dinner. And here she was, panting, out of breath, and desperate to stay alive. All while bonding with evergreens more than she'd ever wished to in her life.

Her mind raced. What could she do now? Wait for dark? Hope she wasn't found? That was probably the smartest thing to do. Then she could make her way to the police station. There was no way that Uncle Chris had infiltrated the local police!

But then there was Zeke. A new panic rose in Lainey Jo's throat. If whoever was after her got to the truck, they would get to her backpack and, in turn, find the pink cat. Lainey Jo squeezed her eyes shut as she curled into the shrub. Maybe that was for the best. Whatever the reason, let Uncle Chris and his lackeys have the silly toy.

Hadn't she given enough to stop him and his trafficking business? Hadn't she sacrificed her life to protect the innocent? God had to give her a break, an opening. He promised hope and a future, didn't He? The idea that this could be her life, always running, always afraid—

Lainey Jo couldn't stifle her shriek as hands grabbed her ankles and dragged her from beneath the evergreen canopy she had hoped hid her.

She launched forward, her hands extended, fingers like claws. She would not hesitate to dig the man's eyes out this time. But he was prepared. A well-executed flip and roll, and Lainey Jo found herself flat on her stomach, arms pinned behind her back. The weight of the man pressed down on her, and his breath was hot on her ear.

"Don't make a sound!"

Bowen!

Lainey Jo stiffened, twisting her head to try to look over her shoulder. She couldn't see his face, but she could smell his scent, and in a brief second, Bowen had flipped her onto her back.

Anger was not the word to describe the emotion in his eyes.

"Get up," he hissed.

Lainey Jo obeyed. She had no other choice and at the moment *wanted* no other choice.

Bowen led her across the park, his pace so swift she tripped trying to keep up with him.

"Where are we going?" she asked.

He didn't answer.

He was furious.

Lainey Jo couldn't blame him. She would be too, had she been in his shoes, but at least she'd understand the motivation for the actions taken. To protect him. To protect Pax and Gramma Lou. That had to count for something, didn't it?

They hurried up a grassy embankment to an SUV she'd never seen before. It was tan with tan seats and a brown steering wheel. Bowen yanked open the door.

"Get in."

Lainey Jo scrambled into the seat and he slammed the door shut. Rounding the vehicle, Bowen climbed into the driver's seat and in a few seconds, they sped forward. He took an on-ramp, which gave them access to the highway she'd run across not fifteen minutes earlier.

She looked at Bowen. She hated to bring it up, but she had to. "The truck—my backpack—I have the stuffed cat in it."

Bowen's jaw was set. A muscle twitched in his cheek. He didn't look at her. "We already retrieved it."

We.

That meant Pax had come too. He probably had Zeke as well. Or maybe they'd just abandoned Zeke since it was so obviously tied to them.

She felt sick. Nauseated. Her head pounded. Lainey Jo slouched in her seat.

The silence between them was palpable. Stark. Dangerous.

Lainey Jo knew she was going to have to explain her actions, and as justified as she believed herself to be, she had a strong inkling that Bowen would still not find it acceptable.

Never in all of his missions had Bowen ever felt such a sense of absolute fear as when he'd spotted Lainey Jo sprinting across the highway. Especially when he caught sight of the man behind her, who seemed to rethink his options and darted off back into the alley. There was nothing Bowen could do either. He was stuck on the highway, and the chance sighting could only be credited to God. There was no other way Bowen could have stumbled across Lainey Jo at the perfect time. But it was obvious she'd been found, and who knew what had transpired.

He'd managed to catch an exit and get to the park. Now, he could feel Lainey Jo trembling beside him in the SUV he'd borrowed from a local contact who'd hooked him up. Pax had sent him a text moments before Bowen had spotted Lainey Jo, saying that he'd found Zeke outside the store.

It was as they'd both guessed. Lainey Jo had gone for a burner phone. She was going to call the marshals. He couldn't blame her, and he had a pretty good idea why she'd done it. Bowen admired her motives to keep them all safe, but it had been a dumb move nonetheless. She was blessed to be alive.

Lainey Jo leaned against the door, clutching the seat belt like it was her lifeline. He noticed a lone tear trickle down her cheek. He'd also already taken into account the scrapes on her palms, the bruising at her neck and the way she carefully moved her head. It was more than apparent there'd been an intense wrestling match. Part of him admired the fact she'd escaped. The other part was filled with such a hot fury that Bowen wasn't sure what to do with it.

All he knew was the guy who'd run back into the alley better pray he never came face to face with Bowen. Ever.

"I'm not going to say 'I'm sorry.'" Lainey Jo's small voice wobbled with unshed tears.

Still, Bowen was impressed by the spunk she had to defy him. Unsure of his own emotions at the moment, he bit his tongue. He didn't want to say something cutting, but if Lainey Jo had been one of the guys on the team, he would have lit into her so hard she'd be emotional pulp by the time he was done.

But what right did he have to hold her accountable for misjudgment? After his own errors on the last mission with Pax? Bowen had never considered himself blessed to be alive. It should've been him who'd taken the bullet that day. Not the woman they'd been trying to extract and get to safety. All because of his pride. His arrogance. His own confounded idea that he was a machine, not a man.

Pax should have disowned him. But he hadn't. That was how the brotherhood worked. They'd all made justifications for Bowen, and maybe they were right on some level. But still…

Bowen bit back a sigh. Yeah. He had no right to ream Lainey Jo out.

The road was clear ahead of them. He checked his mirrors. They weren't being followed.

Fine. He'd opt for a different tactic.

"Are you all right?" Bowen made sure his voice was calm and even. At Lainey Jo's glance, he must have been successful. She seemed surprised that he wasn't going off like an IED on her.

"I—" She swiped at her face.

Ahh. More tears. She was trying to hide them now.

Bowen suppressed a surge of admiration for her quiet strength.

"I'm fine," Lainey Jo concluded.

"What happened?"

She eyed him for a second, and Bowen kept his attention trained on the road ahead and behind him. Finally, Lainey Jo cleared her throat. A few minutes later, Bowen believed he had the gist of what had happened, along with her reasoning for it.

"I didn't think you'd come after me." Her conclusion surprised him.

"Why wouldn't I?" Bowen had no intention of telling her about the conversation he and Pax had after Pax called him when he spotted Lainey Jo taking off in Zeke. Neither of them had felt forgiving in the moment. But duty was more important than how they felt. Now, he even *felt* relieved he'd gone after her. He was going to have to think on that later.

"Because. It's obvious I was trying to get away from you all." Lainey Jo looked sideways at him. "Although, I guess I did steal your truck."

"Call it 'borrowed' and I'll let it go."

She managed a small smile. "Fine. I *borrowed* your truck."

"Did you get in contact with the marshals?" He needed to know where things stood.

"No." Lainey Jo shook her head. "I had just gotten the phone and then—I guess I'm not that great at avoiding being found."

"E and E is a skill," Bowen admitted. That was one of

the things any aspiring SEAL learned in training. As a whole, it was SERE training. Survival, evasion, resistance, and escape.

"Am I in hostile territory?" Lainey Jo's attempt at humor didn't slip past Bowen.

He raised his brow and shot her a quick grimace. "Eh, hostile enough."

"He wants the toy cat," Lainey Jo said. She'd already mentioned it, but Bowen was glad she'd brought it up again. The truth of it hung like a weight between them. It needed to be discussed.

"He give you any idea as to why?"

"No." Lainey Jo shook her head. "But, Bowen?"

His name on her lips gave him a little start. He ignored it. He was already controlling his blood pressure, his heart rate, and his senses. He didn't need to add an undefined counterattack of a romantic nature.

"Yeah?" It was a safe response, so Bowen opted for it.

"We need to rip it apart. We need to see if there's anything hidden inside of it."

That had been his original plan. But first, he had left Lainey Jo in what he thought was safety in order to get a different vehicle and retrieve Gramma Lou. He'd succeeded at the first and was halfway back to the safe house when Pax had called.

Gramma Lou was there now. And, assuming *she* didn't get any wild ideas, in the next thirty minutes Bowen would have both women in the hunting cabin. Momentary safety if nothing else. Then he could recalibrate with Pax. Figure out what it was about that pink, furry cat that was so important. And hopefully, keep avoiding the fact that a growing part of him just wanted to pull Lainey Jo into the circle of his arms to keep her safe.

* * *

"Don't you say a word about being sorry," Gramma Lou instructed as she ushered Lainey Jo into the cabin. She didn't seem to care that two navy SEALs were glowering at them, arms crossed over their chests. Instead, she pulled Lainey Jo into a warm embrace without even asking. For a second, Lainey Jo was stunned. She couldn't say the last time she'd received an actual hug from anyone.

She must have stiffened because Gramma Lou began to loosen her grip. Lainey Jo was quick to reciprocate the embrace, and for one more precious moment, they stood drawing comfort after a horrific day.

This time, as the older woman released Lainey Jo, she addressed Bowen and Pax.

"I made cheesecake brownies this afternoon and managed to snatch them before Bowen kidnapped me and brought me here." Gramma Lou didn't bother apologizing for the sass in her tone. "Now you two, wash up before you have dinner, and then we can break those bars out and the sugar might actually sweeten you both up a bit."

Pax was the first to smile, Lainey Jo noticed. He dropped a kiss on Gramma Lou's cheek.

"Ahh, you're the best, *Mami*." His Latino accent thickened, and Gramma Lou shook her finger at him.

"Make sure your friend over there knows that."

They both shifted attention to Bowen, whose tight expression changed to one of resignation.

"You know I think you're the best, Gram."

She moved to her grandson and patted his cheek. "I know. And I love you for it, you brute." There was nothing but sheer affection in her moniker, and Lainey Jo noticed Bowen's eyes soften significantly.

"I'll eat later," Pax said. He was stuffing a cheesecake

brownie into his mouth, obviously ignoring the idea of a full meal. "I'll take first watch."

"Thanks." Bowen nodded.

The two men exchanged looks, and Pax exited the cabin.

Lainey Jo wasn't sure if she should be remarkably uncomfortable or relieved. She was back in relative safety, but with zero answers and a heap load of trouble she'd caused the men. As for Gramma Lou...

"I'm so sorry you've gotten dragged into this." Lainey Jo's apology was met with a wave of a hand.

Gramma Lou returned to the table and began setting out paper plates. "Never you mind about that. At my age, a little adventure is a good thing. All I ever do is cook and bake." She lifted her eyes. "And you should be grateful," she added. "If Bowen hadn't brought me here, you'd be eating dehydrated green beans and pineapple for supper. Instead, we have cold pasta salad and salami sandwiches." Gramma Lou pulled two containers from a cooler and dropped them on the table. "Bowen said I'm not allowed to start the woodstove to cook."

Lainey Jo was still compiling what to say as she hungrily eyed the food. Bowen managed it for her.

"Only you would be able to pack supper, bring dessert and manage to collect your things in a three-minute extraction." Bowen snagged a sandwich, not bothering to sit down. He took a bite.

"You taught me efficiency." She swiped the sandwich from his hand with a stern look. "Now sit down and pray."

Lainey Jo bit back a smile. Watching Gramma Lou with Bowen put the SEAL in an entirely different perspective. He suddenly didn't seem so fierce. It almost wasn't hard to imagine him as a little boy running around under his grandmother's feet.

She grew serious at the thought that raced through her mind. It must have been so worrisome to have Bowen gone for months on covert operations with no word. The bond between them was so obviously strong.

They made quick work of supper—and that was about five minutes for Bowen, Lainey Jo calculated. She was still scooping her third forkful of pasta salad into her mouth when he turned to her.

"Where's the cat?"

"The cat?" Gramma Lou lifted her gaze. "We have a cat?"

"A toy cat," Bowen explained.

"Real ones are nicer," Gramma Lou interjected.

"We're not getting a cat." Bowen rolled his eyes.

"Don't use that tone with me." Gramma Lou grinned, poking her fork in his direction. She laughed then and finished with, "Okay, I'll be quiet and let you do your thing."

"Thank you." Bowen's look of affection was not lost on Lainey Jo. She wondered what it would be like if he gave her a similar one.

Her face heated as he raised his brows.

Oh yes. He was waiting for an answer.

She looked to the cot where her backpack had been set. "It's in there. Pax brought it inside."

Bowen stood and took mere seconds to extricate the toy from its pack. He slid his fixed-blade knife from its clip attached to his pants and lofted it over the toy.

"Good gravy!" Gramma Lou dropped her fork. "Are you going to kill it?"

"It's not alive, Gram." Bowen sliced the blade along the side seam of the cat.

Lainey Jo sat in silence. There was no way she wanted to admit the sudden surge of emotion as she watched Bowen cut into the stuffed toy. She remembered the day Uncle Chris had given it to her. She remembered how it'd sat on her bed every day until nighttime. She remembered how, as she grew into adulthood, the cat had been one of the last remaining carryovers from childhood.

It had been a last grasp for what had been, she supposed, and that's why she'd taken it when she went into the program. Then she'd forgotten about it in its obvious hiding spot in the cookie jar. Now?

Bowen opened the seam and pulled at the innards. He paused and moved to a position over the table.

"Hand me a clean plate?" he asked.

Lainey Jo reached for the pile of paper plates nearest her and retrieved one.

Bowen set the toy on it and proceeded to relieve it of the stuffing. First, there was the expected white polyester fill that Lainey Jo had always pictured being inside stuffed animals. But soon, as the stomach on the cat deflated with no obvious answer as to why it was important, Bowen spilled out the tiny foam beads that filled its paws. The stuffing collected on the plate, and then, in a swift flop, a thumb drive followed.

It landed on a pile of beads and fill.

"Where did—" She stopped. She knew exactly where it had come from if someone were to answer her literally. "Who? Why?" Lainey Jo couldn't form a complete sentence.

Bowen didn't seem to notice, and Gramma Lou was respectfully quiet. He lifted the thumb drive. "I'm going to take a wild stab that whatever is on this drive is what your uncle's men are after."

EIGHT

"I promise you, I had no idea that was there."

Bowen studied Lainey Jo and had to accept she was telling the truth. There was nothing but utter shock on her face, and she didn't seem to be able to tear her eyes from the thumb drive.

"How did it even get inside the cat?" Bewilderment laced her voice.

Bowen set the now emaciated stuffed cat on the table, but kept the thumb drive held between his thumb and index finger. He turned it over, assessing both sides. It was unmarked.

"You said your uncle gave the cat to you?"

Lainey Jo nodded. "Yes, but—" She lifted her eyes to meet his. "Was that in there since I was a kid?"

He couldn't answer that question. Probably neither of them could. At least not until they saw what was on the drive.

Gramma Lou had grown quiet now, all of her jesting aside. It was as though she could sense the seriousness of the discovery and respected the gravity of it.

Bowen turned the thumb drive over once more. "There are no markings on it. No way to tell who it belongs to."

"Uncle Chris," Lainey Jo stated in no uncertain terms. "I know it's his. It has to be. There's no other explanation."

He wasn't sure he would state it quite so emphatically,

but Bowen had to admit everything was pointing toward that conclusion.

"We need to see what's on the drive," he stated.

"I don't have a computer."

He offered Lainey Jo a reassuring smile. "It's okay. I've got my laptop." Retrieving it from his duffel bag, he pulled out a chair at the table and opened it. Pressing the power button, he waited for the device to boot up.

Lainey Jo pulled her chair around next to his to share the view of the thumb drive's content. A tickle of unease ran through him. It wasn't one of warning or impending trouble, it was purely from the fact that he could almost feel the bare skin of Lainey Jo's arm. The way she avoided touching him by keeping just enough platonic distance between them made his nerves stand on end. She was dressed in a T-shirt and blue jeans. Nothing extraordinary. But for a brief moment, as the laptop took its grand ol' time to fire up, he was struck by the fact that she was the first woman in ages that had heightened his senses in a way that most men would find pleasant. Enticing. Even tempting.

"Are you going to enter your password?"

Lainey Jo's simple request alerted him to the fact that he'd allowed his mind to wander, and the laptop welcome screen was glowing back at him.

"Yeah," he grunted. As he entered his password, his eyes met Gramma Lou's above the computer screen as she stood across from them on the other side of the table. There was a twinkle in her eye. She looked from him to Lainey Jo and then back to him. A small smile teased her mouth.

Bowen raised one eyebrow in stern warning.

Don't go there, Gram.

But it was too late. He might be able to warn his grandmother from entertaining romantic notions, but Bowen was afraid he'd already relinquished more territory in that region of his mind than he'd prepared for.

The computer ready, Bowen plugged in the thumb drive and then navigated to its content.

"I'm nervous," Lainey Jo admitted.

He didn't answer. Mostly because he was tongue-tied at the moment and willing himself to focus on the task at hand.

Lainey Jo shifted. This time her arm brushed his.

He removed his left arm from where it rested on the table and tried to make a subtle edge away from her. Lainey Jo didn't seem to notice.

A box popped up on the screen.

"Fantastic," Bowen muttered. But he wasn't surprised.

"Why isn't it opening the drive?" Lainey Jo leaned closer to the computer as if her presence nearer the screen—and him—would somehow have an effect.

"It's encrypted." Bowen's statement of the fact didn't change the outcome. They would get it open, it was just going to take more time.

"Can you get it unsealed?" Gramma Lou interjected.

Bowen glanced between the two women. "I can't, but I would guess Pax might be able to. He did some time with cyber-security. If it's poorly implemented encryption or older, he may be able to hack it."

"Should I go get him?" Lainey Jo asked.

Bowen blinked, raising his brows in disbelief that she'd even asked.

Lainey Jo shrank back, and guilt riddled him. He had to remember what the woman had been through over the last two days. The last few years. His ability to be sensitive was poorly lacking.

"No. When I relieve him on watch, I'll let him know. He can take a look at it."

"That could be hours." Lainey Jo was getting desperate.

Bowen nodded. "Yes, but we can't force it open. Unless you know how to hack an encrypted thumb drive."

He'd done it again.

Lainey Jo pulled away this time, moving her chair back to where it had been.

Bowen sensed her absence immediately.

Gramma Lou cleared her throat as if she'd gotten something stuck in it and set to work cleaning up the counter that was already spick-and-span.

Bowen tried again. "Listen, we have to do things systematically. I don't want to mess around with the drive and screw anything up. We'll leave Pax to keep watch, and when he comes in I'll—"

"I know." Lainey Jo pushed up from her chair and stalked to the window. The curtain was drawn, and she reached for it to pull it back.

"Lainey Jo!"

Bowen didn't regret the sharpness in his voice, only because circumstances called for extreme caution. He'd already coached her that windows were off limits. Still, he did regret the way Lainey Jo's entire body jerked in startled surprise, and she dropped her hand like the curtain was on fire.

He moved to his feet.

Lainey Jo held out her hands, her eyes wide. "I get it. Never mind. I didn't mean to look out the window. I didn't mean—any of this."

"I never said it was your fault," he countered.

"You didn't have to." Lainey Jo wrapped her arms around herself. "I know this is my uncle and my problem.

I dragged you and—all of you—" she looked to Gramma Lou "—into this and now I can't even give you answers."

"We'll get them. We just need to take it slow."

"We need to call the marshals," she retorted, challenge in her expression.

Bowen drew in a controlled breath. "We don't know if we can trust them."

"That's crazy talk," Lainey Jo spat back.

Bowen hated to admit it, but in the moment of temper, she became even more attractive.

"If we can't trust the US Marshals, then way more people than me are in trouble."

"I didn't mean the entire branch of service, Lainey Jo. We don't know if someone tied to your case is somehow in connection with your uncle's ring."

"The entire trafficking ring was supposedly disbanded," Lainey Jo pushed back. "It doesn't exist."

"Obviously, that's not entirely true," Bowen challenged.

"So then we need to get the law involved!" Lainey Jo's voice had risen an octave, whether in anger or desperation, Bowen wasn't sure.

"I agree." He tried to reassure her. "But not until we know what's on the drive. Not until we know exactly who we can trust."

"So until then, we're stuck here? I'm a prisoner here?"

Tears. There were the tears. Welling up in her eyes like the nemesis that would do him in quicker than a sniper's bullet.

"You're not a prisoner, Lainey Jo." Bowen softened his voice.

She stared at him in disbelief. "But I am. I've been a captive since the moment I turned witness against my uncle. He's freer in prison than I am in Witness Protection."

A tear trailed down her cheek, and Bowen noticed the

scrapes from her attack earlier in the day were beginning to bruise. Her eyes were peaked. Exhaustion was creeping into every visible part of her body.

In that moment, he didn't care that Gramma Lou was discreetly making herself busy in the kitchen behind him. He didn't care that he was a SEAL who had the emotional empathy of a bear. He didn't even care that only three days ago, he'd been keeping himself busy with no clear purpose in life.

All he knew right now was that Lainey Jo needed to be held.

There was only one man available to do the job.

She had not expected this. The reassuring warmth, the strength in his arms, the broad chest, and especially the way Bowen Mays pulled her into himself. Lainey Jo was trembling. Emotion and exhaustion had taken their last toll on her, and it was all she could do to stay standing. Now, Bowen held her, and she didn't even have the stamina to refuse. Instead, Lainey Jo wrapped her arms around him, her hands gripping his olive-green T-shirt against his back.

In another time and another place, she might revel in the hardness of his muscular frame. She might even become a bit intoxicated by the scent of pine and spicy musk that emanated from him. But tonight? She was only vaguely aware of it. Instead, comfort was coming from the last person Lainey Jo had expected. If Gramma Lou had crossed the floor as quickly as Bowen had, she wouldn't have been surprised. But this was different. This was a protective gesture. Reassuring, yes, but mostly protective. His arms encased her like a guardian.

"We're going to figure this out." His words were spoken against her temple, and she felt his warm breath on her skin.

Did it matter to him that she was crying? That her tears wet his shirtfront? She hoped not, because there wasn't any stopping them. It was as though a floodgate had been opened, and for the first time since Uncle Chris went to trial, someone had reached out to her with intentional care.

"I'm so tired," she mumbled into his shirt.

"I know." Bowen fell silent. Lainey Jo wondered if it was because he was a man of few words, or if he was struggling to find the right thing to say. She wouldn't blame him if it were the latter. A few days ago, they had no clue the other existed. Now, it seemed as though they'd been shoved together and clung out of sheer necessity. It was no wonder that Bowen was at a loss to know what to say.

But he surprised her. His hand came up and he pushed hair away from her face, tucking it behind her ear. "You need to sleep. That's the first thing you need to do."

"But—" Lainey Jo lifted her head. She tried to look toward the table. To the laptop. The thumb drive.

"It will wait." Bowen shifted so he stood between her and her line of sight.

She met his gaze.

"Trust me," he said. It wasn't a command, and it wasn't a plea either. It was an ask. A promise that he didn't regret being involved in her chaos and that he had every intention of seeing it through.

Lainey Jo nodded, straining against the temptation to lay her head back on his chest. Bowen pulled away, but kept his hands on her upper arms. His head bent, he captured her attention with those sky-blue eyes that held so much confidence and intensity. Lainey Jo was pretty sure that if Bowen went up against her uncle, Bowen would come out the winner.

"Go get some sleep." He tipped his head toward the cot.

"Pax and I are on watch. Gramma Lou is here." Bowen shifted, and this time his movement was purposeful in bringing Gramma Lou into the conversation.

She must have been hovering, waiting for the invitation. The woman hurried forward and, to Lainey Jo's disappointment, Bowen shifted her into Gramma Lou's care.

"Come, honey."

Lainey Jo followed Gramma Lou across the room, but not without a backward glance at Bowen, who smiled reassuringly and then returned to the table and his laptop. With his back to her, Lainey Jo shifted her attention to Gramma Lou's ministrations.

"You crawl into bed." Gramma Lou pulled the covers back, and Lainey Jo didn't hesitate to climb in, clothes and all.

Gramma Lou tucked the covers around Lainey Jo as though she were a child. Her hand smoothed Lainey Jo's hair, and she leaned over her and planted a soft kiss to Lainey Jo's temple. "Oh, honey," Gramma Lou murmured. "You rest. The Lord will keep you in safety. He's given you to us."

Lainey Jo clung to those words. She held onto the idea that God had seen fit to bring her to Bowen's truck that first time. That He had seen fit to bring her to Gramma Lou's home. That He had managed to include Pax, who had a hunting cabin out in the no-man's lands of Wyoming's Bighorn Mountains.

Yes. Even while being shot at and attacked, here she was. For now, safe. For now, she could rest.

Lainey Jo's soft breathing assured Bowen she was asleep.
Gramma Lou slid a cup of hot coffee across the table to-

ward him and then took her seat, cupping her hands around her own mug.

Bowen didn't like the way she watched him. He kept his attention on his laptop, which was a pointless endeavor. The screen kept reminding him that he was not going to gain quick access to the thumb drive.

"You're ignoring me." Gramma Lou kept her voice low so as not to disturb Lainey Jo.

"You noticed, huh?" Bowen made a pretense of moving the cursor on the screen.

"Of course, I noticed." There was a soft laugh in her voice. "I've taken care of you since you were in diapers. You can't fool me."

"I know." He hoped his grandmother would let go from there, but he knew her well enough to expect differently. He was right.

"It's not your responsibility to carry the burden of saving Lainey Jo."

Ouch. Gramma Lou's declaration, delivered with soft authority, made him lift his eyes. Hers were the same blue as his own. He knew this because he'd grown up with everyone telling him how much he looked like his Gramma Lou. She had raised him. After his parents divorced, his father left their lives, and his mom lived until he was twelve. When breast cancer took her, the only person he had left was Gramma Lou. She wasn't a woman to mince her words, and at times, he'd joked with his team that if they were to send Gramma Lou in, the mission would be over before it began.

"Bowen?" She pressed now, requiring him to answer.

"I have to keep her safe." He matched his grandmother's decisive tone.

"I never said you didn't. I merely said it wasn't your

responsibility to bear the weight of it. That is for God to bear. He will clear your path. You just have to follow and be His hands and feet."

She'd always said that. Even in her letters he'd received while on duty.

Be His hands and feet.

That was his job. To complete the mission assigned. Whether God gave it to him or the United States Government, failure was not an option.

The silence was thick between them.

Gramma Lou finally broke it. "It wasn't your fault, you know."

He looked up sharply. "Gram."

She frowned. "No. No, you've carried this since you were discharged. Now you're taking it with you into your current situation with Lainey Jo. God has given you the gift to be a protector, Bowen, but He didn't give you complete control over situations."

"I know that." And he did. He just didn't like it.

"Then you can't blame yourself when it doesn't go the way you planned."

"Mission failure is mission failure."

"And yes, missions fail," Gramma Lou retorted.

But she didn't know. She couldn't understand. They didn't train to fail. They didn't spend hours beating their bodies into submission to accept defeat. A SEAL went into each mission with the intent to succeed.

But it didn't help when a soldier sabotaged their mission due to their own stupidity. Gramma Lou could say whatever she wanted, but in the end, if he didn't stay aware—if he didn't maintain control over every aspect—there would be a repeat.

And the last thing that Bowen was willing to do was to

lose Lainey Jo. She deserved more than a failed mission. She deserved to live.

He was going to make sure that happened. With or without the good Lord.

Lainey Jo lay still, careful not to move, but she could hear the conversation between Bowen and Gramma Lou. Her heart ached at the vulnerable pain in Bowen's voice. She didn't know his story, but it was clear his history as a SEAL and his current position in life were very much intertwined.

When Lainey Jo heard a door close, she dared to lift her head and look up from her position on the cot. Nighttime had fully set in, and she saw Gramma Lou at the table, enveloped in a soft glow from a camping lantern. She was observing Lainey Jo, and their eyes met.

"Don't mind him, Lainey Jo." Gramma Lou's gentle voice filled the cabin. "He's been troubled for a long time."

Lainey Jo saw no point in pretending to sleep any longer. She sat up, glancing around to verify that Bowen had indeed gone outside. Probably to relieve Pax from his watch. She had limited time with Gramma Lou, and she didn't want to waste it.

Moving to the table, she sat down in the chair Bowen had abandoned. It wasn't her business, but she asked anyway. "What happened to Bowen?"

Gramma Lou drew in a deep breath, weighed with the heaviness of love and ache for the hurt in her grandson. She turned her coffee mug in her hands, its bottom scraping on the table.

"He was discharged due to an injury that disabled him permanently for active military duty."

Lainey Jo digested this. Bowen didn't appear injured.

Gramma Lou must have realized her confusion. "He had an injury to his back on his last mission. He's mostly healed now, and it's not very noticeable, but it bothers him from time to time, and it disqualified him."

"How did it happen?"

"I don't know all the details, and I'm not sure I ever will. But Bowen's team was sent to rescue an American woman held hostage by hostiles in the Middle East somewhere. Because of his injury during the mission, Bowen wasn't able to provide adequate cover for the woman. She ended up killed."

"Oh." Lainey Jo's heart sank. She'd not expected that. For some reason, Bowen seemed like a superhero. One that was haunted by his faults and perceived failures, but one who would come out a conqueror heroically in the end.

Gramma Lou continued. "Paxton was injured on the same mission. He took a bullet, and it also ended his active duty status. He took a medical discharge along with Bowen. But Pax has taken it far better than Bowen did."

Lainey Jo considered for a moment, then dared to ask, "Why do you think that is?"

Gramma Lou met her gaze. "Because Pax was doing his duty and carried no personal blame for what happened. But Bowen saw the mission as a fiasco. He shouldered the responsibility for it."

"But why? How does he think it's his fault?"

Gramma Lou blinked rapidly, and Lainey Jo wondered if the woman was going to cry. She didn't. She only sniffed and tapped her coffee mug with her finger. "He'd hate it if I told you," she admitted.

Lainey Jo could understand that. Bowen wasn't the type who would want his personal business discussed. But it would help her understand him, and right now, that seemed important.

"I won't hold it against him, whatever it is."

Gramma Lou gave her a sharp look. "No one holds it against him. Only he does. Bowen failed to report over a month's worth of insomnia caused by post-traumatic stress. He went into the mission severely sleep-deprived, and he believes if he had been more on his game, the mission wouldn't have failed."

"Is he right?" Lainey Jo asked.

Gramma Lou shrugged. "The navy didn't seem to think so. They stated other reasons for the mission's failure. But it doesn't matter. Bowen is Bowen. He shoulders responsibility not just for what happened, but for Pax, and even for his own career. That boy was born to be a SEAL."

"He still is one," Lainey Jo replied reverently.

Gramma Lou's smile was wobbly this time. "Yes. But he doesn't see himself as worthy of the title."

Lainey Jo debated for only a few seconds before standing up.

"Where are you going?" Gramma Lou lifted worried eyes.

"He's outside?" Lainey Jo asked.

"Yes, but—"

She hurried to the door, knowing full well Bowen would not approve of her leaving the cabin. But it was dark. She would be difficult to see. Pax was standing guard. Bowen needed her.

Lainey Jo didn't have to go far. He stood at the edge of the slanting, slatboard porch, staring out into the night, a pair of binoculars held to his eyes.

"I told you not to come outside."

So he knew it was her? Lainey Jo didn't care. She was

filled with a sudden need, a sudden necessity, to see Bowen. To reassure him. But how did she reassure a navy SEAL? Weren't they made of such fierce stuff that they were virtually impenetrable?

But no. That couldn't be true.

"Go back inside." His directive was ordered firmly but without any sharpness.

"It's dark out. No one can see me and—" Lainey Jo started.

Bowen turned. She could see a tortured expression on his features, even though the darkness was doing a good job of hiding most of it. It quickly dissipated at the sight of her. "Night vision." He lifted his binoculars. "If they have a pair of binos like these, you might as well be standing under the sun itself."

"I'd melt if I were that close to the sun," Lainey Jo whispered. She suddenly felt brave even under his glower. Tonight, she had witnessed a truth about Bowen Mays. For all his grunt and grit, he was more like Mr. Rogers than he realized. He might bear the moniker from his buddies as a joke, but Bowen was softhearted deep inside. He craved to protect others, and when he failed, for whatever reason, he personalized it.

Bowen stepped toward her. "Go inside. Please, Lainey Jo."

Lainey Jo looked up at him in the darkness. He was standing closer than she thought even he had planned. She saw his chest rise and fall as he breathed. "I want you to know, whatever happens to me, I would never hold you responsible."

An undefinable look crossed his face. He didn't answer.

Lainey Jo dared to continue. "You can only do what you can do for me. The rest is in God's hands."

Did she even believe that? The question challenged her, and in that brief moment, Lainey Jo chose to trust the truth of her statement.

"I won't let anything happen to you," Bowen promised. He raised his hand, brushing her cheek with the back of his fingers.

Her breath caught in her throat, his motion stealing words from her for only a second. But she had to speak. She had to release him from his self-imposed sense of duty to her. "You can't promise that, Bowen," she whispered. "You can do your best, but in the end, whatever happens, it's not your responsibility."

Bowen lowered his hand. He leaned forward and for a wild moment, Lainey Jo thought he might kiss her. Press his lips to hers in gratefulness for her freeing him from the weight of it all. But instead, his arm reached around and behind her, twisting the doorknob to the cabin and pushing the door open a few inches.

His breath was warm on her ear as he leaned in. "I don't forgive myself when there's mission failure. I won't forgive myself if it happens again. Now go inside, Tadpole, before I make you for your own safety."

None of it was delivered harshly. His words were more of a caress mingled with an aching wistfulness that somehow he could actually believe what she said.

Lainey Jo nodded, breathless. She should have known it would take more than just a few words from her to release a man haunted by the traumas of war. Because, regardless of the circumstances, that's what it was. A war. And it wasn't over yet.

NINE

"I got it!" Pax's announcement, as the morning sunlight snuck under the crack of the front door, startled both Lainey Jo and Gramma Lou.

The door swung open simultaneously as Bowen entered. Lainey Jo noted his face was drawn, serious, and with his nighttime gear on, including sidearm and who knows what else strapped to his chest, the only thing missing was camouflage face paint.

"I got it!" Pax pounded the table, directing a victorious grin Bowen's way.

Bowen rested a rifle against the wall as he closed the door behind him. "The files?"

"Affirmative."

Lainey Jo and Gramma Lou exchanged looks. Now was the moment of truth. Why Uncle Chris was after the thumb drive to begin with, and more importantly, why he was after her.

Pax addressed Bowen. "It was a bit tricky, but the encryption was old. I'll spare you the details. But we're in."

Bowen leaned his hands on the table, arms extended as he hovered next to Pax. He shot a glance at Lainey Jo and tipped his head, encouraging her to join them.

"Let's open it," he said.

Lainey Jo did as she'd been instructed, but her feet felt heavy. Her heart thudded against her chest, and she couldn't shake the sensation that everything she believed even now to be true was about to be upended.

Gramma Lou maintained her distance, sitting down on a chair across the room to give them space. Lainey Jo had a feeling that she was praying, and while it brought Lainey Jo some comfort, she honestly thought she was going to need more than prayers in a few moments.

With Bowen on his left and Lainey Jo on his right, Pax looked between them, his fingers hovering over the laptop's keyboard.

"Ready?"

"Do it," Lainey Jo answered.

Pax clicked on a file folder, and it opened. Document files appeared, and then, toward the bottom of the folder, were image files.

"There." Bowen pointed. "Photographs. What are those?"

Lainey Jo gripped the table. Reliving the nightmare that had been the trial for Uncle Chris was not something she wanted to do. But she had little choice.

She recalled the photographs taken by the FBI after she'd given them information on how to track Uncle Chris and his patterns. They were photographs of him with key men in his organization. Pictures of some of the young women the FBI had rescued in a raid.

Documents could remain innocuous, but photos were a visual condemnation.

"Here goes," Pax said, and clicked on the first photo.

The window popped open, and a picture of Uncle Chris filled the screen. His handsome, thirty-something-ish face like she remembered from when she was eight. Dark brown hair, deep-set eyes, chiseled jaw. He had always seemed a little bit like Superman, until he turned into her story's villain.

"Who's that?" Bowen asked her.

"Uncle Chris." Lainey Jo could hear her voice, small and tight with emotion.

The photo showed her uncle standing outside the metal door of a brick building she recognized from the trial as being one they funneled drugs through. Drugs that financed the trafficking, which in turn, financed who knows what all.

The next picture was Uncle Chris and two of the main henchmen who worked alongside of him.

Lainey Jo felt a small bit of relief. These weren't new revelations to her. She pointed at the screen to explain. "That guy there was Uncle Chris's right hand in their drug operation. The other guy acted as an accountant."

"You know all this from the trial?" Bowen inquired.

Lainey Jo nodded.

Pax clicked on the next photo.

Lainey Jo froze. She stared at the man in the picture, a new wave of trepidation washing over her. "That—that doesn't make sense."

"Who is it?" Bowen asked.

Lainey Jo didn't answer. She couldn't. The face was so familiar. Too familiar. It didn't belong here. The man was standing outside the same building.

"Lainey Jo?" Bowen pressed.

"What's the next photo?" she asked Pax, who clicked, and a new one sprang up. It was worse. This time, the same man was shaking hands with Uncle Chris's cohorts. It was more than apparent they knew each other, and in one hand, the accountant was extending a manila envelope folded into a thick rectangular form that looked exactly like an encased wad of cash.

"Lainey Jo, who is it?"

She still couldn't answer, but she sensed Bowen's mounting impatience. How did she explain what she couldn't even explain to herself? The graying brown hair, features that weren't terribly unlike her own, the well-tailored suit, the wedding ring on his left hand.

Lainey Jo sensed all eyes on her, waiting for her answer. She couldn't hide it from them. There was no reason to, and it may help explain what was going on. But how? How did it explain anything? It only made her more confused.

"Can you tell who it is?" Pax's request was delivered more gently than Bowen's.

Lainey Jo looked down at him. There was a platonic concern in his dark brown eyes. She lifted her gaze and locked eyes with Bowen. His icy blue ones looked ready to go to war—on her behalf.

"It's—my father."

There. She'd said it. She'd said it aloud, and it had only made her feel worse.

"Your father?" Bowen shifted his attention back to the screen. "I didn't think he was indicted alongside your uncle."

"He wasn't. He wasn't part of Uncle Chris's organization." Desperation mounted inside of her to clear her dad's name. "The FBI even did an investigation. Dad released all his files to them. Nothing of Uncle Chris's illegal dealings could be traced to Dad."

"And yet, there he is exchanging *something* with your uncle and his men."

Paxton's observation only mounted the tension inside of Lainey Jo.

"It doesn't mean anything," she argued. "That photo was taken years ago. Maybe—maybe Uncle Chris was blackmailing Dad into being quiet about stuff he knew!" It was a frantic grasp at hope.

"That doesn't make sense. That guy there," Pax pointed to the accountant, "is handing your dad something, not the other way around. Whatever it is, it was given *to* your father. It's not your dad paying someone off."

Lainey Jo bit the inside of her bottom lip. She shot a look behind her at Gramma Lou, who sat still, her eyes wide in empathy. She gave Lainey Jo an encouraging smile thick with regret.

Even Gramma Lou believed Lainey Jo's father was guilty of something!

Lainey Jo reared back. "No. There's got to be more to explain this!"

Pax clicked on the next few pictures. All of them were subsequent photos of the hand-off of the envelope, her father taking it, her father getting into a black Mercedes, and then a random photo of her father outside of his office on his phone as he got into a car that Lainey Jo didn't recognize.

"That's all of the pictures," Pax stated.

"See?" Lainey Jo met Bowen's eyes, silently begging him not to jump to conclusions. "Those pictures don't prove anything."

Bowen opened his mouth to reply, but Pax interrupted.

"This might, though. There's a voice file here. It's a recording of something."

Lainey Jo stilled. She didn't want to hear it. If it was her father's voice—if there was evidence there that somehow linked Dad to Uncle Chris's trafficking ring—her entire world, or what little she had left of it, would crumble. The implications were obvious to her, even if Bowen and the rest weren't aware of them yet.

If the data on this thumb drive was proof that her father—Scott Ludlow—was part of the trafficking ring, then of course Uncle Chris would want the drive. Because it meant he had been the family's scapegoat for the entire operation, had been burdened with the blame of it, and Dad had evaded it all.

What was worse was that if this was evidence that Dad was involved, there was a possibility the trafficking business wasn't completely obliterated by the FBI's investigation. It might not have even been entirely shut down!

Her father's voice filled the cabin.

Pax had clicked on the recording.

As she listened, Lainey Jo's knees gave out. She grabbed for the table, and Pax was quick to pull a chair behind her. Lainey Jo looked at Bowen. His expression was grave, as well it should be.

It was instructions. All of the recording was instructions from Scott Ludlow to his brother, Chris. Within a minute, it became abundantly clear.

Uncle Chris wasn't the head of the trafficking organization.

Scott Ludlow was.

And Lainey Jo's father had gotten away with it, while Uncle Chris took 100 percent of the fall.

Bowen watched Lainey Jo as she sank onto the chair. All the color had leaked from her face, and he could hardly blame her. The evidence was incriminating. It was a sure-fire conviction if it ever found its way to a court. No wonder her uncle was after it. If he had taken the fall for the entire criminal organization, then this was the evidence he'd need to bring down his brother, Scott. Lainey Jo's father. It sounded to Bowen as though Scott Ludlow had carefully crafted everything to be unattached to him and point all the blame at his brother. Now his brother—Uncle Chris—wanted to see Lainey Jo's father taken to task. He would not be the family scapegoat.

The recording ended.

Silence pervaded the cabin.

What could anyone say? Bowen was at a loss for words. It all made sense now. The reason Lainey Jo's apartment had been ransacked, the reason someone had shot at her. They needed her dead, so she was no longer in the way, and they needed the drive that Chris had probably hidden in the stuffed toy years ago just in case something went wrong.

"Your father is—"

Lainey Jo held up a hand, stopping Pax midsentence.

Pax looked at Bowen, who gave a short shake of his head.

"Lainey Jo," Bowen tried. "Have you had any communication with your father since you went into WITSEC?"

She shook her head. "No."

Bowen was distracted for a moment as Gramma Lou motioned that she was going to make coffee. Her answer for everything. He nodded and shifted his attention back to Lainey Jo.

"And you've never seen any of this before?"

"No!" Lainey Jo's voice rose. She glared at him, but Bowen didn't blame her. "My father was cleared of everything. Nothing tied back to him."

"That's how he wanted it," Pax observed.

"Or maybe—" Lainey Jo was desperate to find a different conclusion. Bowen could almost see her wheels turning. "Dad might have—maybe when this was recorded, he was working with the FBI, and he was trying to get Uncle Chris to say stuff to incriminate himself. And so it was all a ruse on Dad's part, and—"

"You don't believe that." Bowen stated the truth, because that's what it was. There was zero logic to her rambling attempt to exonerate her father. Unfortunately, the sooner she accepted it, the sooner they could get her to safety.

Lainey Jo eyed him. "I also don't believe my father had anything to do with *trafficking* human beings."

"Probably not directly," Bowen agreed. "But this is clear evidence, Lainey Jo. That voice recording proves he was the head of it. Not your uncle. Your uncle was the second to your father."

"He couldn't be!" Lainey Jo protested.

Bowen knew she didn't want to believe it, and probably didn't even want to consider it.

Gramma Lou cleared her throat.

Bowen shot a look of gratefulness. He'd be happy to hand the emotional comforting to her. But instead, Gramma Lou surprised him.

"I think sometimes the hardest things to accept in life are when those we love the most disappoint us."

"This is more than disappointment." Lainey Jo sucked in a shuddering breath. "It's betrayal." She rounded Pax's chair and stood next to Bowen. "You have to believe me— my father wouldn't—he *couldn't*—" She bit off her words.

Bowen didn't want to say it. He didn't want to be the one to remind her, but the truth was, she'd probably felt the same way about her Uncle Chris a few years ago when his sins came into the light. He wouldn't argue with anyone that a father's sins would be harder to reconcile, but they also couldn't be ignored.

Paxton and Gramma Lou remained dishearteningly silent. They were really going to leave it to Bowen to reason with Lainey Jo? Bowen shot Pax a look. That was Pax's job. He was the sensitive one. He was the one to calm the hysterical. But he was no help now. He kept his head purposefully averted, almost as if he felt like he were intruding on a private moment.

Bowen tried again. "You're not responsible for your father's choices."

Lainey Jo's eyes widened. "You think that's what I'm upset about? I *know* I'm not. But—if this is true, then my father has put me in an impossible situation!"

Bowen nodded. He knew exactly where her mind was taking her, and she wasn't wrong.

"I have the evidence that incriminates my dad. If I destroy it, it all goes away."

Pax's head jerked up. "You're not destroying it."

"I know!" Lainey Jo ran her hand over her forehead in agitation. "But I don't want to turn it into the authorities! I'll be condemning my own father! Don't you think it was hard enough to do against my uncle? Now my dad?"

Bowen reached for her, lightly gripping her upper arms and capturing her attention. "You're not responsible for your father's failures."

"But I am responsible if I turn that over to the FBI. He'll go away for—for *life*. My entire family—my mom—they'll be ruined. It was bad enough with Uncle Chris. The Ludlows won't recover from it. They'll all hate me."

Bowen didn't know what to say. She was right. There was no reconciling it.

"I'm sorry." It was all he could say. He moved his hands up and down her arms, attempting to comfort her.

Lainey Jo shrugged away from his touch.

Pax coughed.

Gramma Lou took a step toward them as though she wanted to say something.

Bowen cast her a pleading look.

Please, say something wise.

But Gramma Lou just steepled her fingers over her mouth and shook her head. "I'm so sorry, honey." Tears brimmed in Gram's eyes. Bowen looked to Lainey Jo. Tears were in hers as well.

"Yeah." Pax's voice carried through the room. "This stinks."

Lainey Jo dropped her head into her hands. "I don't know what to do."

Bowen hated being the realist. But they needed to be objective now. There would be time to deal with emotions later, and with both him and Pax in the cabin, no one was on watch right now. He'd come in intending to swap with Pax, but the files had distracted him.

There were no bones about it. They needed to get back on task.

"We need to get the files to the FBI. I'll turn them in." Bowen met Lainey Jo's gaze. "That way you don't have to."

She bit her lip, her chin quivering.

Pax spoke up. "I'll make a copy first. When we get Internet access, I can upload it to a secure drive. We don't want just one copy out there, and we don't want it stored on equipment that could get damaged. Then you can take care of it."

"We need to figure out how to get it into the right hands, too." Bowen still hadn't shaken the idea that Marshal Halloway had been murdered shortly after setting up a meeting with Lainey Jo. Bowen wasn't a conspiracy theorist, but he also knew some could be bought to turn sides, and if someone was working inside the marshals or the FBI and they'd turned on Halloway, they'd be as persistent to get the drive as Chris Ludlow.

"If we head to my place, I can take the drive and—"

Pax's plan was interrupted as a piercing shot shattered the cabin window. The bullet slammed into the far wall.

"Down! Down! Down!" Bowen shouted. He flew toward Lainey Jo, tackling her to the floor.

He heard Gramma Lou cry out and saw Pax pulling her to safety in the corner behind the iron stove.

"We need to get them out of here!" Pax yelled.

They were pinned down. Bowen eyed the window where the first shot had whizzed through the glass. The curtain had been moved—probably by someone passing by and inadvertently brushing it. But it was open enough for anyone with a rifle and scope to get a look into the cabin. They were just blessed that the bullet had missed them. Bowen noted the bullet impact on the far wall. Without calculating the trajectory, he would guess it had been meant for Lainey Jo. Once again, they'd missed.

He breathed a quick prayer of thanks for God's intervention.

Their plans were shot. Literally. Getting the evidence to the authorities was going to be a lot harder now. They'd been found. Their cover was blown. And Lainey Jo was still the primary target.

TEN

Lainey Jo squirmed under Bowen's weight. He lifted off but kept his hand on her shoulder, holding her down.

"Don't move," he said.

"I'll take the drive." Pax had already crawled across the floor and snatched the thumb drive from the laptop.

Bowen maneuvered to his rifle, which he'd leaned against the wall. Lainey Jo noticed him take a quick inventory of his gear. He patted his sidearm and his knife. He gave Pax a sharp nod.

"Take the drive, take Gramma Lou. I'll cover you. Head out the back door. You parked your truck there, yeah?"

"Yeah. One out front, one out back like we planned." Pax looked annoyed rather than panicked. "And right before I was going to get my morning coffee!"

"Bad timing, yeah?" Bowen snarked back.

Lainey Jo, lying flat on the floor, exchanged looks with Gramma Lou, who was on the other side of the table in the same position.

"When we take off, we'll divert the shooter." Pax lowered himself by Gramma Lou, and Lainey Jo watched as he coached her through the next steps.

Bowen spun his body and positioned himself below the window.

"Let me know when you're ready," he tossed over his shoulder at Pax.

"You ready?" Pax reached for Gramma Lou's hand.

Lainey Jo wanted to cry out. She wanted to tell Gramma Lou to be safe. But her words were stuck in her throat. Fear had all but paralyzed her, and all she could do was pray that Pax could get her and the thumb drive to safety.

"If there's more than one shooter—" Pax started.

"I know. We'll have to go through the back door," Bowen shot back.

"There won't be a truck there."

"We'll head for the trees. Then we can circle around."

Lainey Jo noticed the men exchange a few hand signals. She had no idea what they were saying, but she had no choice but to trust them.

"Let's do this." Pax moved for Gramma Lou.

At the same time, Bowen lifted his rifle and shot a few rounds out the window.

The sound vibrated through Lainey Jo's body, stinging her ears. She covered them with her hands, pressing her face into the floor. She didn't dare move. If she stood up, she'd be shot. Or worse. She eyed the back door. In the few seconds it took for Bowen to get his shots off, Pax had hustled Gramma Lou out the back door. She heard the truck rev as the engine started.

Another gunshot.

"Stay down!" Bowen's command was unnecessary.

Lainey Jo closed her eyes as he shot another few rounds.

She heard gravel flying as Pax took off in his truck. A bullet sounded like it hit somewhere outside the cabin.

"Are they shooting at Gramma Lou?" Lainey Jo cried, lifting her head out of instinct.

"Get down!" Bowen ordered.

He answered with a few more shots. "Pax got them out of here."

Relief surged through Lainey Jo.

Bowen slid across the floor and leveled down beside her. He commandeered her attention, the intensity in his expression one she had no intention of arguing with.

"We're going to go out the back door. We need to make a run for the hill behind us. There's an outcropping and some trees. It's got cover."

"What do we do then?" She wanted to be aware and be helpful. She didn't need to be more weight on Bowen's shoulder by being completely lost.

"One move at a time, Tadpole." He winked. He shook two fingers at the back door. "We have to move quickly in case the second guy is here too. Sniper out front means the other could come around. We'd be boxed in. You ready?"

No. She wasn't ready in the slightest. But Lainey Jo nodded.

"When I say 'go,' you go. Don't look back, don't wait for me. I'm going to cover us. You fix your eyes on the outcropping and get behind it. You understand?"

The fervency in his eyes was mixed with concern.

"I'll be okay. I got it," Lainey Jo said with more confidence than she felt.

"All right. Let's do this."

The next few moments made Lainey Jo's blood race and her pulse pound. She heard Bowen's command to go, and she scrambled to her feet, bolting for the back door. Lainey Jo could hear Bowen behind her, and without thinking, she looked over her shoulder. He was moving with his back to her, his gun pointed toward the cabin. But somehow he knew she'd hesitated.

"Go!" he shouted.

This time, Lainey Jo ducked her head down and sprinted up the hill. The grass snagged at her ankles, but the junipers gave her some cover as she dodged behind them. The rock outcropping was at least fifty yards ahead, and the terrain was steeper than she'd expected.

Lainey Jo's breath hitched as she surged up the hillside. She heard a few shots.

There were no shouts from Bowen, but as instructed, Lainey Jo kept her head down and made for the shelter behind the boulders. When she reached them, Lainey Jo fell to her knees behind them, scurrying on the ground until she was pressing her back against the cold security of the rock.

Bowen threw himself next to her, cradling his gun. "You good?"

She nodded.

"Okay." He seemed to weigh his options for a few seconds, and then he leaned toward her, keeping his voice low. "There's no way we can get to the SUV. The sniper will pin us down. I'm going to need to circle around and see if I can come up behind him."

"But what about the other shooter?" Lainey Jo panted, still out of breath from her streak up the hill.

"There's only one shooter. Right now, at least. If I can take out the sniper, we can get to the SUV."

"What do I do?" Lainey Jo wanted to help. She eyed Bowen's pistol.

His smile was crooked as he read her thoughts. "No. You're staying put. As long as you stay down, he can't get a shot."

"What about you?"

Their eyes locked.

"Me?" Bowen gave a short laugh. "This is old school,

Tadpole." With those words he shuffled to the other end of the outcropping, ready to make his move. "Stay put, stay—"

"Stay low. I got it." Lainey Jo managed a nervous smile.

Bowen gifted her with a quick nod and then was gone.

It seemed like hours. Probably, it was only minutes. Maybe even seconds. Lainey Jo had no idea. All she knew was that her back was to a rock outcropping and she was looking up the hill behind her. The grass beneath her was green, and thankfully, as the slope extended upward, the trees were thicker, intermingled with more rock outcroppings. Lodgepole pines grew thicker the higher she looked. Their narrow, round trunks and thick evergreen branches seemed to stand sentinel. She could hear water in the distance. A creek, probably, but she could not explore the natural beauty of the area around the cabin. It was regrettable. If she wasn't terrified for her life—and Bowen's—she could see hiking up the slope at a leisurely pace. Looking over the vastness of the forestland that made up the Bighorn Mountains. But instead, she was trying to control her breaths. Even they sounded loud to her.

There were no more gunshots. She had no idea where Bowen was. Was it awful that she was waiting to hear one solo shot that would indicate he'd taken out the sniper? Probably. Yes. That was awful. But everything about this situation was horrid.

And it was her father's fault.

That reality slammed into Lainey Jo once again.

Her father. There was no denying what she'd seen, but even more, what she'd heard on the recording. Instructions for the next shipment. A head count of the "girls." And then a conversation about money and the exchanging of "inventory" into different hands.

It was nauseating. Her father. He had been so broken by Uncle Chris's betrayal—at least he'd appeared to be. What was worse was that this new evidence on the thumb drive that Pax and Gramma Lou had escaped with in no way released Uncle Chris from guilt. It merely compounded the family guilt.

She was caught in the middle of the two men who had meant the most to her growing up.

Lainey Jo sucked in a breath, willing tears away. Now was not the time. She had to keep her wits about her until she and Bowen were safe.

Movement up the hill captured Lainey Jo's attention. She stilled, holding her breath. Hopefully it was just a moose or an antelope, but her gut told her that with the gunshots earlier, wildlife like that would be long gone.

Danger creeping into her blood, Lainey Jo hunkered down, hoping to make herself smaller. She squinted through the pines.

Yes.

There.

A man ducked behind a boulder.

She could tell it wasn't Bowen. The man wore black, like her attacker in the alleyway. That meant—realization hit her. This probably wasn't the sniper Bowen was circling around to confront. This had to be the second guy. The one who preferred up close and personal. Who had sneered into her face and slammed his fist into her shoulder.

So far, it didn't seem as though he'd seen her, but Lainey Jo knew if she stayed where she was, he would. She had to move somewhere she wasn't exposed from behind.

Lainey Jo scanned her surroundings. She could try to find more shelter where the lodgepoles grew thicker. There was some underbrush, but the higher she would climb, the thinner it would get.

She caught sight of the man again. He had woven his way around. He was hunting Bowen! He had to be. There was no question he was moving in the direction Bowen had gone. Lainey Jo strained to come up with something she could do to divert the man's attention from Bowen. But without knowing for sure if he was after Bowen, she'd only be drawing his attention to her, and she had no idea where she was supposed to go from here.

This wasn't in her arsenal of skills. Hiding. Taking shelter in the wilderness. Her tennis shoes were made of canvas, not hiking materials. She had been raised going on vacations on yachts, meandering the walkways of Paris, and sipping espresso at an Italian piazza. This new Lainey Jo? She was merely a cover. In reality, she was still Lainey Jo Ludlow. The woman who had given testimony in the court of law. She was an ill-prepared woman with a false identity, who had adapted to life in Wyoming only because the Witness Protection Program had placed her there. For certain, the mountains just outside of her new home held no enticement to her. They were expansive, intimidating and reminded her of the territory she'd had to traverse during the trial. An unknown wilderness filled with unpredictable dangers.

Now, more than ever, Lainey Jo wished she hadn't led such a pampered life. She wished she had even a smidgeon of Bowen's skill set and ability to assess a dangerous situation. Instead, she was hiding behind a rock, a deadly enemy in view, with no idea where to run.

Lainey Jo managed to get to her feet, staying low in a squat. The only options she had were to stay where she was and pray her attacker didn't see her, or take off for the trees and hope she could find a good place to hide.

The latter seemed smarter, but also very unpredictable.

Making up her mind, Lainey Jo began to slink along the outcropping, keeping it to the left of her body and shielding herself from the direction of the cabin. She eyed the trees, making out a shadowy area that looked to be a collection of boulders and ground covering. She'd head for that, and hope, and pray.

Not wanting to lose sight of the enemy, Lainey Jo paused before she made a run for it. She scanned the area where she'd last seen him, but her vision came up empty.

Where had he gone?

Anxiety pumped adrenaline through Lainey Jo's body. Had her assailant already left the area? Should she stay put? Or was he winding his way down closer to her and an inevitable confrontation?

Lainey Jo didn't have time to consider all the answers. A movement, then a swath of black, and then, less than a hundred yards away, she saw him. The man from the alley. He gripped a gun in his hand, and in that moment, Lainey Jo knew he'd spotted her.

Panic overwhelmed her and spurred Lainey Jo into action. She dove forward, no longer worrying about keeping a low profile, just about reaching the cover of the trees. But with the man so close, there was no way she had enough distance between them to find a place to hide successfully. He'd be on her in a minute.

Lainey Jo's tennis shoes and their smooth bottoms were no match for the rugged terrain. Her left foot slipped, and she crumpled to the ground, catching herself on a small sapling that grew up from the earth.

She could hear him breaking through branches.

She couldn't hesitate. He'd kill her if she did.

Inspired by necessity, Lainey Jo took off at a dead run

in the direction Bowen had gone. She pushed off a tree and dodged another branch as she managed to make it into the grove of pines.

The shout behind her was unintelligible, but it told Lainey Jo she couldn't slow her pace.

She scrambled up part of an embankment, surprised by the existence of a patch of shale rock that scattered beneath her feet. Lainey Jo looked frantically behind her. He was coming! She could make out his expression now. He was intent, and he was catching up.

Lainey Jo spun back, and as she did so, her shoe slid again. This time, Lainey Jo was knocked off balance, and she fell onto her hip, the shale beneath her giving way. She cried out as she slipped down the embankment. Desperate to stop, Lainey Jo stuck out her foot, but it snagged on a tree root that jutted up from the ground.

The last thing she knew was the ground was up and the sky was down, and the pain of her body hitting the earth was enough to make her world go dark.

Lainey Jo's body felt bruised, and her vision was blurry as she opened her eyes. She saw clouds above her. Blue sky. A bird winged its way across her sight, swooping and floating like a black silhouette. She was lying flat on her back, the surface beneath her cold and ridged.

It started coming back to her. The cabin. Bowen. Pax taking off with Gramma Lou and the thumb drive. The man.

Lainey Jo scrambled to move her hands and sit up, but she was met with instant resistance. She lifted her hands and saw they were zip-tied together, not so tight as to cut off her circulation, but enough that she could not wiggle them free.

She rolled onto her side, ignoring the pounding in her

head. A truck bed. She was in a truck bed. The deep green paint was scraped and scarred. There was nothing else in the truck's bed, so Lainey Jo pushed against a wheel well to scoot into a sitting position. The truck was pulled deep into the forest. She couldn't see a road or any buildings, and the geography, while similar to where the hunting cabin had been, was definitely not the same area.

Lainey Jo heard him before she saw him. The movement of someone approaching the truck. She struggled with her wrist restraints even as she noted her ankles were not bound. The plastic of the ties dug into her skin. They were impossible to break. Determining to get away, she shoved herself onto her knees. A few more gymnastics and she'd be on her feet and could leap over the side of the truck.

But there wasn't enough time. Earth crunched beneath her captor's feet. She heard him clear his throat. Lainey Jo looked around the truck bed, hoping there was something she could weaponize that she hadn't noticed before. But there wasn't.

Lainey Jo managed to brace her elbows on the side of the truck in order to leverage it and get into a standing position. But then, he was there. Standing in front of her. His face had a blank expression. His eyes were fathomless and secretive.

"Uncle Chris?" Her hoarse gasp was met with his tight smile.

"Hello, Lainey Jo."

The shooter had vanished.

Bowen had scouted the entire area, and aside from bullet casings and the imprint in the ground from the rifle's tripod, there was no sign of the would-be killer.

He growled deep in his chest. The worst part about this

situation was the variables that were unaccounted for. The unknowns of who exactly was after Lainey Jo, the question of how they'd found them here, and then the bigger issue of getting Lainey Jo to safety.

Bowen didn't discount that the shooter could still be anywhere. It was dangerous being out here, and even more dangerous running solo. He was grateful Pax had been able to get Gram to safety along with the drive, but he'd give anything for his teammate to be beside him. The complications were getting more intense.

They were out in the mountains too, so calling anyone was out of the question without a SAT phone. Which he had. Just not on him. And who was he going to call? At this point, Bowen was beginning to question his caution against the marshals. Lainey Jo was right. There was a good chance someone had tapped Marshal Halloway's phone. Just as good a chance as there was of someone on the inside doling out information that got him killed. But the idea of handing Lainey Jo over to anyone aside from himself brought a worry into his gut that he wasn't accustomed to.

Maybe he was overexaggerating because of his past failure. Maybe it had made him too protective, too emotionally invested, and off his game. Whatever it was, he didn't like that he didn't have a clear directive. And he needed one. Now.

He wove his way back toward where he'd left Lainey Jo, scanning his surroundings as he hiked. Once he got back to her, he was going to make their way to the SUV and head to a predetermined rendezvous point. He and Pax had identified it earlier, for just this situation. They'd hook back up there and then get the thumb drive—and Lainey Jo—into safe hands.

Uneasiness began to creep over Bowen as he drew near

the area where he'd last seen Lainey Jo. Birds were restless, evidence of a disturbance. If Lainey Jo were still hunkered down where she was supposed to be, the wildlife wouldn't be bothered. He dodged behind a tight grouping of pines and slung his rifle over his shoulder. Withdrawing his pistol, he grasped it with familiarity.

Something was off.

Bowen chanced to look around the safety of the trees.

Nothing.

A flock of blackbirds cawed in the treetops. They were upset. Some intrusion had ruined their peace.

Bowen snuck diagonally across the grove of lodgepole pines. He noted the earth was disturbed in one of the steeper sections of the embankment. Shale had been pushed downward, two skid marks in the earth where someone had slid.

Lainey Jo.

Why had she left her position?

Bowen had to make certain that was the case before he acted on a wrong assumption. Weaving a cautious way through the trees, Bowen came out at a higher point that looked down on the outcropping Lainey Jo was supposed to be tucked behind.

She wasn't there.

He'd expected that, but her absence filled him with an unwelcome foreboding. She had promised to stay put and stay low. She'd even finished the instructions for him. Bowen couldn't imagine what would have made her move in the height of such danger unless she'd been forced to.

Which meant someone had gone after her!

Bowen didn't abandon his caution, but he moved at a quicker pace. Once he made it to the outcropping, he studied the ground for evidence of where Lainey Jo had gone. He could see by marks in the earth, she had taken off at a run. A little further, he met back up where the shale had been disturbed.

A small mound of black grabbed his attention, and Bowen moved toward it. He scooped it up from where it lay on the ground. It was a black stocking cap. Nondescript with no patch or logo embroidered to identify it. But it was definitely not Lainey Jo's.

Bowen fisted it in his hand.

The shooter had either skirted him and gotten to Lainey Jo, or this belonged to the second guy who preferred up close and personal interactions—as evidenced by Marshal Halloway's death.

Either way, it wasn't a good sign.

Bowen traced the skid marks to where it was apparent the person who had slipped collided with a rock. He bent and picked up a few strands of long hair that were stuck to the rock.

Lainey Jo's.

It had to be.

Which meant either someone had taken her, or she was on the run. But it was the evidence of scuffed earth and broken underbrush that worried him the most. The signs pointed toward someone hauling something heavy through the woods. It also told him that as much as he wanted to believe Lainey Jo had gotten away and was still hiding somewhere, he was likely wrong.

She had come face to face with her killer.

And Bowen had failed to protect once again.

ELEVEN

Nothing had prepared Lainey Jo to come face to face with Uncle Chris. Aside from the fact they'd had zero interaction since she turned witness against him, he was supposed to be in prison! Not here. Not in the Bighorns, looking at her with an unreadable expression.

She eyed him warily, falling onto her backside and pushing against the truck bed with her feet to put distance between her and her uncle.

"H-how?" she asked.

Uncle Chris lifted his hands and made a motion for her to calm down. He looked over his shoulder, then back to her.

"You need to be quiet, Lainey Jo."

"Quiet? What do you mean?" Lainey Jo rolled onto her knees now that she was on the opposite side of the truck. Her hands throbbed from the plastic strips binding them. Her head felt like it was in a vise, and she had a feeling there was a little blood crusting on her cheek from a scrape to her face. She must have tumbled when she'd slipped down the shale.

The man in black had been chasing her, and—

"You're not him." Lainey Jo stared at her uncle. "Where's the man who was chasing me?"

Uncle Chris gripped the side of the truck.

Lainey Jo noticed his hands were rough and not the carefully manicured ones that they had once been.

"That's why you need to be quiet." Uncle Chris motioned to her hands. "And if you behave, I'll cut your restraints."

"You tied me up?"

"I didn't want you to strike out at me when you woke and I—" another nervous glance into the woods "—I needed to take care of things."

"Things?" Lainey Jo didn't even want to know, and yet she felt she had to. For her own safety. "Where's the man who was chasing me?"

"I don't know. I was trying to find him." Uncle Chris motioned for her to come back toward him. He pulled out a knife from his pocket and flipped it open. "I'll cut your ties."

She wanted to trust him, but she didn't. "How are you out of prison?"

Uncle Chris leveled a cynical smile at her. "You prefer I'm there, don't you?"

"It's where you belong," she spat.

If she could stand up and get onto the wheel well on this side of the truck, she could jump to the ground. She'd have to run into the woods to escape, and worse than before, now she had no idea where she was. For all she knew, she'd been out for over an hour and Uncle Chris had driven to some secluded area nowhere near the hunting cabin.

"Maybe I do." He shrugged, seemingly unoffended by Lainey Jo's derision. "But for now, Lainey Jo, I'm here to protect you." He waved his fingers. "Come here. Let me get you loose and then get into the cab."

"I'm not going anywhere with you."

A shadow of frustration flickered across Uncle Chris's face. "Don't be stupid. You know I wouldn't hurt you."

"Do I?" She reared back, her voice rising in surprise. "You've had someone trying to kill me for the last few days. I've been shot at and attacked. You've threatened my friends, my security—now you want me to trust you?"

"Be quiet!" he hissed. "You're going to get us killed!"

"I thought *you* were the one doing the killing." Lainey Jo hedged as she pushed herself into a sitting position on the wheel.

Uncle Chris's face darkened. "You don't want to do that."

Lainey Jo eyed him. "I don't trust you."

"I don't trust *you*." Her uncle didn't mince his words. "You betrayed me, the family—but that's beside the point at the moment. That man is going to come back, and if we don't get out of here, he's going to kill us both."

"Kill us *both*?" Lainey Jo shook her head and then regretted it. "I will not be manipulated by you anymore, Uncle Chris." She launched herself over the side of the truck. Her plan was smoother than her landing. With her hands tied, Lainey Jo had no way to balance herself, and she fell to the ground.

In a quick motion, she rolled away from the truck, clambering to her feet. Uncle Chris rounded the truck, his scowl the picture of a man infuriated.

Lainey Jo pushed herself to her feet and took off into the woods. She had never imagined how hard it was to run with her hands tied, but now she knew. She managed to dart through the trees and to the edge of a hill that led down to a creek. It flowed with a beautiful rolling current, creating white riffles around rocks and a stony shoreline. Lainey Jo skipped down the side of the hill, this time expecting the ground beneath her to be loose and unsteady. But she could hear Uncle Chris behind her. He didn't shout her name or call for her to stop, but the crashing of his body through the trees told her that he was gaining faster than she was moving.

She barely made it to level ground when her uncle slammed into her, tackling her to the earth.

Lainey Jo twisted and fought. "Let go of me!" Her shout echoed and alerted birds that protested as they fled from their perches on the tops of the pines.

"Shut up!" Uncle Chris's slap of his hand stung. It connected with her cheek, and for a blinding moment the slap merged into a vision of light pricks and stabbing pain.

Uncle Chris bent close to her face, urgency etched in the corners of his eyes. "I'm sorry. But you need to be quiet. I told you—you're going to get us both killed."

"What are you talking about?" Lainey Jo whimpered. Tears ran down her face now, even though everything inside of her willed herself to be strong and not to let her uncle see her weakness.

"I know you think I'm the one trying to kill you, but I'm not. All those shots that missed? That was me. Trying to get the man in black off your back, and trying to keep you from getting killed."

"*You* shot at me? You're the sniper?" Lainey Jo stared incredulously at her uncle.

"Sniper might be too complimentary for me, but yes. I never meant to actually kill you. They were *warning* shots."

"You shot me in the head!" Lainey Jo spat.

"Grazed you. And that was accidental. Just—that's not important right now. What is, is that I need your stuffed cat—the one I gave you years ago. It's my insurance against your father. I hid a drive inside it. Just give me the cat, Lainey Jo. Before he gets here and kills us both. I already chased after him in the woods and got you to safety."

"Why don't I feel very safe?" Lainey Jo glowered.

"Knock it off!" Uncle Chris hissed. "Don't you know he's the man your father hired to kill us? Both of us. He wants us dead, Lainey Jo. I have evidence on that thumb drive. Your father knows you'll turn witness again. If you don't let me help you, we're both dead."

Somehow, she knew Uncle Chris was telling the truth. While every ounce of her soul wanted to believe better of her father, wanted to believe he'd never do something so heinous as to put out a hit on her and Uncle Chris, she knew it was true.

Lainey Jo squirmed beneath her uncle's hold. "Let me up."

He moved off of her, and Lainey Jo rolled to her backside.

"You won't run?" Uncle Chris had taken out his knife again.

"No. I won't run." It was a lie. If she had the opportunity, she would. Bowen didn't know where she was. *She* didn't know where she was. As she considered it, she realized Bowen had no idea that one of the shooters was her own uncle, who was supposed to be behind bars.

Lainey Jo held out her wrists, and Uncle Chris sliced through the restraints. She rubbed a hand over each wrist, willing feeling and relief back into them.

"I need that drive, Lainey Jo. I need your stuffed cat." Uncle Chris was on his knees as they stayed in their positions on the forest floor.

The creek rippled and rolled next to them, a rhythmic peace that contrasted against the pounding urgency of the situation.

Lainey Jo pulled her knees up to her chin. Her hands were throbbing, and her head felt like it might explode. If she needed to run, she had to get her wits about her.

"I don't have it." She prayed Pax had gotten it to safety. At this point, she prayed he'd even had the foresight to contact the authorities.

"You have to understand." Uncle Chris was growing agitated. He raked his hand through his peppery hair. It had gotten more gray since Lainey Jo had last seen him in the courtroom. "I knew for years that if anything happened, I would take the fall. Your dad and I—we make good partners, because we're smart and our skills make us powerful. But there's no trust between us. I knew your dad had taken careful measures to make sure he was in the clear. We'd planned it that way for one thing. If something went down, we didn't want the entire organization to go with it. So I'd be the scapegoat, and your dad would get me out via legal maneuvers. That was the plan. At least, how it was *supposed* to happen."

"But Dad didn't carry through with it," Lainey Jo stated.

"Exactly. Scott has plenty of people in high places. With some payments under the table, evidence could have gone missing, and even some of your testimony could have been debunked. But your dad let it all go. He let me take the fall so he could walk away with absolutely zero repercussions. He made no effort to fulfill what we'd always planned. He wanted it all for himself, and this was an ideal way to get me out of his way."

"And that's why you'd made the thumb drive?" It didn't take Lainey Jo much to put those pieces together. "You hid it with an eight-year-old kid." Nice. She stared at her uncle in disbelief.

"I knew my brother well enough to know years ago that I should always have a contingency plan. Scott's priority is himself. Then me. If I get between him and his own preservation, I'm expendable." Uncle Chris rubbed his eyes, evidence of his frustration and mental exhaustion. "I'd made a voice recording without Scott knowing before there was even a hint that we were going to be investigated. Just to have something in case I ever needed it. I had pictures taken covertly. The documents I copied from Scott's computer. I put them all on two drives to be safe. One was in your cat. The other, your father got a hold of and destroyed." At Lainey Jo's look, Uncle Chris's brows drew into a scowl. "I had to protect myself. I needed my own insurance."

Lainey Jo readjusted her position on the ground, pulling her hair away from her face and plucking a leaf from the strands.

Uncle Chris eyed her as warily as she did him.

Neither of them trusted each other, and for good reason.

"I never expected you to turn on me, Lainey Jo."

She pressed her lips together to avoid the impulsive "I'm sorry" that was on the tip of her tongue. She couldn't be sorry. Not considering everything her uncle had been a part of, which had ruined lives.

"I looked for the cat since I got out. When I couldn't find it, I knew you had to have taken it with you. You wouldn't get rid of it. I knew that cat meant something to you."

Lainey Jo narrowed her eyes. "It wasn't the cat that meant something to me." Her voice cracked, and she swallowed back her emotion. "It was you."

Uncle Chris jumped to his feet then and stalked a few paces away. He put his palm against the trunk of an aspen, his back to her.

Lainey Jo shifted her position. Once she stood, she would try again. Uncle Chris might outrun her, but even her brief time with Bowen had taught her that she couldn't stop fighting.

Her uncle spun back around. There was pain in his eyes,

evidence that he did feel, that he did have a conscience of some sort. "I had no intention of hurting you, Lainey Jo. I never have."

She gave a little laugh of disbelief. "How can you say that? You knew what you and Dad were doing, and you still encouraged me to work for you."

Uncle Chris lifted his hand as if telling her to stop arguing. "You were as innocent as eighty percent of the rest of our employee base. Most people don't know the company they work for is corrupt. They're never prosecuted. They're not held responsible."

"And you banked on the fact that I would be a part of that eighty percent?" Lainey Jo retorted.

Uncle Chris snorted in derision and planted his hands at his hips, staring at her with a look that insinuated Lainey Jo had no idea of everything that had gone on behind closed doors. "I was trying to protect you from your father. He has no loyalty. Not to me, and not to you." His jaw worked back and forth. "You know what your father did? It was his crowning moment, if I say so myself." The bitterness in Uncle Chris's voice was stark. He didn't even try to disguise the hatred he had for his brother.

Lainey Jo didn't answer, but Uncle Chris continued anyway.

"Scott bribed some of the jury at my trial. He made *sure* that conviction went through." Uncle Chris's eyebrows rose. "And that, my dear girl, is why you retain good lawyers. We were able to obtain enough proof that the jury had been bribed—of course, we couldn't get enough to implicate Scott—but it was enough to get my conviction reversed by a judge."

"That's how you're out of prison," Lainey Jo concluded. "How did I not know this was happening? Why wasn't I kept up to date by the marshals—or moved?" Not as though Uncle Chris would have the answers to that, but it seemed like an obvious no-brainer that if the man she'd taken the stand against and then gone into Witness Protection to be safely away from was going to get out of prison, she would have been at a minimum, notified.

Uncle Chris took a few steps back in her direction.

Lainey Jo regretted asking the question. She needed to be smarter and get him preoccupied somehow. But she also needed answers.

"Your handler—Marshal Halloway—he disseminated the information that you needed to know."

Realization dawned on her, and nausea rolled in her stomach. "You paid him off? He was working for you?"

"I did what I had to do, Lainey Jo, you've got to believe me. Put yourself in my shoes! I searched for the stuffed cat at your parents' place while they were gone. That's when I figured out you'd taken it along. It wasn't on your dresser where it had always been since you were a kid. I didn't expect you to go into WITSEC, and I for sure didn't expect you to take the drive with you!"

"I didn't know anything *about* the drive!" Lainey Jo protested.

Uncle Chris acquiesced with a nod. "Fair. But I had no way to predict you would turn on me and then take on an entirely new identity."

Lainey Jo drew back, glaring at him. "Do *not* blame this on me."

"I'm not."

"So you found out who my handler was and you infiltrated the US Marshals with a bribe?" Lainey Jo concluded. The answer was apparent, but she wanted to hear it. To know without a shadow of a doubt that Uncle Chris was as devious as her father. He thought he was different, but he wasn't.

"Anyone can be bought, and your marshal was no exception."

"Then why did you kill him?" Lainey Jo shot back. "If he was cooperating, why shoot him in the head?" The words sounded so violent as they came from her mouth.

Uncle Chris tipped his head and gave her a look that insinuated she should know the answer to that. When Lainey Jo didn't provide it, he gave it to her. "I didn't kill him. Your dad's hit man did. The same way he killed to find out where you were hidden. The FBI has leaks, and he found them."

"But—" Lainey Jo took the opportunity of the distraction of the conversation to stand. "Does Dad know about the second thumb drive—about my cat?"

"Of course he does," Uncle Chris scoffed. "At least he knows about the drive, just not the stuffed cat. Your dad can find out about anything he wants to, and then he'll take whatever measures he needs to make sure he isn't stained by anything."

"So it was Dad's hired man who ransacked my apartment looking for the thumb drive?" That answered why the cat was still stuffed in the cookie jar. Even if the man had found it, he'd have had no idea the drive was in the cat. Lainey Jo began to put the pieces together. She lifted her eyes to her uncle, in incredulity. "And you shot at me?"

Uncle Chris's expression darkened. "I shot at you to warn you. And it worked. Even today in the cabin."

"But you kept shooting at us." Lainey Jo eyed him skeptically. "When Bowen and I were taking cover, you kept shooting."

"Because I knew your father's man was in the woods.

You went exactly in the direction I thought you needed to go to get further away from him."

"You were steering us with bullets?" Lainey Jo breathed in disbelief. There was no admiration in her voice.

"I was trying to keep you safe."

Lainey Jo remembered Bowen returning fire. In the short time she had known him, she knew it was an act of God that Uncle Chris was still alive. If Bowen had been able to get sight of him, he'd have been dead.

For a moment, Lainey Jo warred within herself. Maybe Uncle Chris really was trying to protect her. She had fled from him, gone into Witness Protection to stay away from him, but all along, it was her father she needed to be afraid of.

Still. In spite of Uncle Chris's twisted justifications, he had still involved her. From the day he'd hidden the thumb drive in her stuffed cat to the moment he'd hired her as his assistant.

For someone who claimed affection for and protectiveness of her, he was remarkably selfish.

Without warning, he lunged at Lainey Jo, gripping her arms in a pinching grasp. "I just want the thumb drive. You go live your life. I don't care. You've done the damage, but it's your father I want to burn."

For a wild moment, Lainey Jo wished she did have the drive. Her father did deserve to be outed. Uncle Chris was free. She knew beyond any shadow of a doubt that his freedom, regardless of his overturned conviction, was somehow the result of money being exchanged. Even an overturned conviction didn't mean immediate release from high-security prison. It couldn't! It meant a potential re-trial, not freedom. Uncle Chris had somehow bought his way out. Paid off more susceptible and greedy black hearts.

But Lainey Jo didn't even care. She wanted to be free of him. Free of her father. If she had the drive, at this moment, Lainey Jo was almost sure she would have thrown it at him.

"Give me the drive, and I'll make sure you're safe from your father." Uncle Chris squeezed her arms painfully.

Lainey Jo knew it was a lie. It had always been a lie. Her childhood had been based on smoke and mirrors. Two men performing the roles of father and doting uncle. Two men who would twist and pull and manipulate the system to serve their greed-filled purposes.

They were evil. They were abusive. They ruined lives, including her own, for the sake of power. She'd been played, and gaslit, and used. While she had no desire to walk down the road of hatred that her uncle was on, Lainey Jo also had no intention of allowing him any further power over her.

Her instinct to live, her will to be free and her strength to do whatever needed to be done took over. She yelled, shoving her uncle hard in his chest. The suddenness of it took Uncle Chris off guard. He stumbled backward, and Lainey Jo pushed him again and he fell over a log that lay behind him.

With a cry of desperation and a prayer of pleading, Lainey Jo sprinted across the creek toward the woods on the other side. The forest was thicker there. The grasses, longer. The undergrowth, bushy and branchy. Her shoes slipped on the stones in the creek, but it was only ankle-deep.

Uncle Chris shouted.

But this time, Lainey Jo didn't look. She would never look back again.

TWELVE

Night was setting in.

Bowen pulled into the rendezvous point he had set up previously with Pax. It was an out-of-the-way campground near a small lake hidden in the wooded region of the Bighorns.

Pax was already there, leaning against his truck, arms crossed. His headlights were off, but his truck was running. When Bowen pulled up, Pax shoved off his truck and approached as Bowen jumped from the SUV.

"Where's Lainey Jo?" Pax's first question was the only thing Bowen wanted to care about at the moment. But first, he had to know.

"Is Gram safe?"

"She's with her pastor and his wife in town. I made sure we weren't followed."

"And the drive?" Bowen asked.

"Safe," was all Pax said. "Where's Lainey Jo?" he repeated.

"I don't know." Bowen was loath to admit it. He clenched his jaw against the fury he felt toward the men chasing her, and also toward himself for failing her.

"What happened?" Pax was to the point, and Bowen appreciated that. He filled Pax in on the details, finishing by brandishing the stocking cap he'd found and stuffed into the cargo pocket of his pants.

"So there were two of them again," Pax concluded.

"Yeah. The sniper—who is either the worst sniper ever, or he's intentionally missing all these times. But then, this proves the other guy was there too. Only I didn't hear him fire any rounds, and I never saw a sign of him." Bowen bit back his anger. He wanted to slam his fist into the side of the SUV, but he didn't. It wouldn't serve any purpose other than potentially busting his hand. He needed his hand.

Pax tugged a device from his pocket and motioned Bowen over. Light from it illuminated Pax's face. It was a GPS, and Pax had pulled up a map of the region. He pointed to a pin he'd dropped on the grid. "There's the hunting cabin. If Lainey Jo didn't escape, but they caught her, then I'd say they either took her deeper into the hills here—" he pointed "—or there's a chance they're leaving the region."

"Why there exactly?" Bowen studied the map and the area Pax had identified.

"There's water. The same creek that runs by the cabin winds its way around there. There's an old trail accessible with a decent truck, but it's not a place you'll run into people. It's a good place to detour if you need to get cover quickly."

"That's our best chance then," Bowen acquiesced. He didn't feel great about it. The mountains were expansive. In a region so vast it wouldn't be hard to disappear. He trusted Pax's intuition, but it was admittedly a shot in the dark.

At this point, Bowen would prefer to have his entire SEAL team on hand. That wasn't an option.

"I alerted the local authorities. Told them about the shoot-out at the cabin." Pax's statement didn't surprise Bowen. It was stupid to go solo on this any longer. But he also knew that the authorities weren't going to move at the speed that was needed. This was way above their pay grade, and by the time the US Marshals and FBI were involved, Lainey Jo could have been taken states away—or she'd be dead.

The last thought spurred Bowen into action. He slapped the hood of the vehicle with decisive force. "We need to get moving."

Pax held up a hand. "Hold on, Mr. Rogers. We're not going in guns blazing like an old Western. You know how this works."

Yes. Yes, he did. Bowen had done rescues and extractions numerous times before. Their success rate was stellar until he'd mucked it up.

Pax ignored Bowen's sullen silence. "We're going to plan this out."

"We have no proof that's where they even are." Bowen hated the fact that he was so helpless. He was accustomed to surveillance, drones, an entire navy behind their missions, not running through the woods like ancient cavemen trying to rescue a damsel in distress from a whack-job psycho.

"Wow." Pax stared at Bowen, his incredulous expression exaggerated by the glow from the GPS.

"Did I say that out loud?" Bowen asked sheepishly.

"*Sí*. You did, *amigo*."

"Sorry."

"Cool your head," Pax admonished. "You know where emotions get you."

"Nowhere good."

"Exactly." Pax eyed him for a moment. His assessment of Bowen's mental and emotional state must have passed. He continued, redirecting his attention to the GPS. "We'll run a sneak and peek first."

Bowen hated the sound of that. "A reconnaissance op is going to take time."

"Yeah. But otherwise we're going in blind—if they're even there."

Bowen blew out a frustrated breath. "We don't have time for this."

"We do this right." Pax was firm. "Get your head on straight. I've never seen you like this."

Bowen growled and jammed his hands against his waist, pacing away a few steps before turning back. "Yeah, man. My head's messed up."

"Lainey Jo is pretty distracting."

Bowen didn't miss Pax's lopsided grin. "Knock it off."

"Why? Deal in reality. A woman finally got to you."

"She's not the first," Bowen muttered.

Pax grew serious. "I'm not talking about our targets. You know that mission was not on you."

Bowen uttered a short laugh. "I cost you your career."

"No. The mission did. And that's a risk to any SEAL at any time."

"I wasn't on my game. I should have reported—"

Pax took three fast strides and gave Bowen a frustrated shove on his chest. "Get over yourself!" There was a dark scowl on his face. "So you hadn't slept in a week. You'd done missions on less before. It was one part of a myriad of unpredictable actions that made things go down the way they did."

"Our target *died.*"

"Because that's how it went down." Pax glared.

"Because I—"

"You think you're it, don't you?" Pax sniffed. "Bowen Mays. Tough guy. Man of the hour. The extractor. What are the rest of us, huh? Your sidekicks?"

Bowen stilled. "No. I—never meant—"

"Then stop bearing the blame for it. We're a team. We're brothers. We move as one, and you know that. Things happen. We both got wounded, and yes, our target was killed. Mission fail. Suck it up. Deal with it. Move on."

Bowen glowered. Pax's words were too close to the truth. He knew if roles were reversed, he'd be saying the same things. Maybe even harsher.

Pax jabbed his finger in the air toward Bowen. "Stop playing God. He never asked you to share His rank. It's why He's the CO and not you."

The words sliced through Bowen with the velocity of a missile. Was that what he'd been doing? Blaming himself as though he'd be the one who had complete control of the situation? Had he put on God's boots and tried to fulfill His duty?

Pax lowered his hand and took on a softer approach. "Do I wish I were still active? Sure, I do. But the navy says otherwise, and that's how it goes. I didn't want a desk job. So I'm here. With my brother. We always said we were going to retire to the mountains. So we got to do it early. Maybe this is exactly where we are supposed to be—for Lainey Jo. Did you ever think of that?"

"But—" Bowen bit off his protest.

Pax knew exactly where he was going with it. "We lost that day. We lost the woman we were trying to protect. It was her time, Bowen. Regardless of what we did, she had a clock on her life, and the alarm went off. Same as you do. Same as I do. When it's time, it's time."

Bowen gave a swift nod. He knew Pax was right. But knowing the truth and adopting the truth were two entirely different things.

Pax wasn't about to let it go. "Now, are you with me?"

"Yeah."

Pax asked again, emphasizing his words. "Are you *with* me?"

"Yes." Bowen straightened. He may not be on his game tonight, but the truth was, Pax's words had stung. Just because he was highly trained, it didn't mean he held the mission in his grip. But this time, it was more personal than ever. It was Lainey Jo. And even though he hadn't known her long, she was already changing him. The impact of the potential of losing her wasn't something he was ready to explore, but he had to be real and admit it was a possibility. He didn't want to accept that. Bowen had a hard time imagining life could go back to any sort of routine now that Lainey Jo had jumped into his truck and into his life.

"We're wasting time." Pax's statement brought Bowen back to earth.

"Let's do this."

"Let's go get your girl." Pax's teasing humor returned.

Bowen couldn't hide the crooked grin that commanded his expression. "Hoo yah!" he stated.

"Hoo yah!" Pax echoed.

Lainey Jo had no sense of where she was. The direction she'd chosen to run in had been purely based on the amount of potential cover she thought she might have. She'd heard Uncle Chris shout. The splashing of water as he'd surged across the creek told her he was fast on her heels. She'd scrambled up a slope and then, on a whim, swerved to the left.

Circle back.

Circle back.

She kept hearing Bowen in her mind as he would use that term. What if she tried it? Or at least her own version of it? Uncle Chris would expect her to keep running away. But if she circled back and crossed the creek, perhaps she could get to his truck and, if God saw fit, even find the keys in the ignition.

It might be too much to hope for, but it wasn't too much to pray for.

Lainey Jo made sure to cut a much wider swath through the woods. Taking her direct path back would have her coming right back into the trajectory of Uncle Chris. No. She needed to parallel the creek for a good while, then cut back and cross it.

Now it was dark. The moon may have been shining, but the cloud covering was thick, and it shielded the moon from shining down on the earth. Lainey Jo wished she could see. Stumbling through the night was laborious. She didn't know the terrain, and she couldn't see it either. Lainey Jo wished the moon could at least light a small path for her, but then, it would also illuminate her presence. If Uncle Chris was behind her, tracking her, then darkness was more likely than not a gift.

Lainey Jo took a moment to sink to the earth. She had to catch her breath. Her legs burned from exertion she was not accustomed to. She'd give anything for some medication, a glass of water and a soft bed.

The idea of peace was far away. Even if she were rescued at this very moment, life was far from being peaceful. She recalled Uncle Chris's claims. That her father had bought off his jury. That her father had hired a hit man to kill them both. The entire concept was so outrageous, Lainey Jo had to force herself to replay every word Uncle Chris had said and weigh it against what she knew.

Had she been so blinded by her father? So trusting of

him that she'd never seen even a warning sign through the entire trial that he might be involved with Uncle Chris?

But no. When the FBI itself cleared her father, there was no reason for Lainey Jo to be suspicious. She had never seen a hint of her father's collaboration with Uncle Chris.

"Don't go into WITSEC, Lainey Jo, what are you thinking?"

Lainey Jo remembered the night she told her father the agreement she'd come to with the FBI. She'd argued that she had to. That Uncle Chris would never forgive her. That her life would be in danger.

"You don't know that!" Scott Ludlow had shoved his whisky glass aside and stood up from behind his desk. He had the same brown eyes as Lainey Jo did, and she saw them snap with emotion. At the time, she'd read it as concern and betrayal. Betrayal by his brother. Anger that Uncle Chris had put Lainey Jo in this position.

"When people get in his way, Dad, Uncle Chris makes sure they disappear. I don't want to be one of those people."

Her argument had stalled her father's.

Now, as Lainey Jo huddled against the trunk of an aspen, she pulled her knees up to her chin, wrapping her arms around her legs. Dad had been silent. For several long minutes. It hadn't been until Lainey Jo had flopped onto a chair opposite his desk and put her face in her hands that he'd spoken.

"I have people. I can protect you."

It made sense, then, his promise. Dad had money. The Ludlow family had power. He could hire an entire security team to follow her around and ensure her safety. As it was, Lainey Jo wasn't unused to at least one bodyguard when she went on travels. Dad always insisted. She assumed it was because they were wealthy and she might be a potential mark for kidnapping and ransom. But it had been such a vague notion. Until now. Now it was worse, and far more probable.

"I don't want to live life like that."

Her argument had been true. The idea of always having her moves watched, logged, reported on—it made her squirm. Uncle Chris might go to prison, and he'd take her along with him. At least, her own sort of prison. Maybe Witness Protection wasn't any different. But at least she'd have a new name, a new home, a new everything.

"You know I can still find you."

When Dad had said that, Lainey Jo had taken comfort in it. The idea that her father was confident enough in his place in life that he could find her, even in Witness Protection, made her feel better. She'd taken it as a sign to go. Because if she ever needed him, or if he ever needed her, Dad would find a way. He always did. He always could. Money made a lot of people talk, and he wasn't averse to using it for those purposes.

In retrospect, Lainey Jo reconsidered his promise.

"You know I can still find you."

He hadn't meant it as a means of protective love and care. She saw that now. It was a veiled threat. One she'd not even been aware of, because she had no reason to think he needed to threaten her.

Dad wasn't involved.

Dad was innocent.

Dad was protecting himself.

Lainey Jo leaned her head back against the tree, closing her eyes against the emotions that swirled within her. Even then, he had been assessing her to see if she knew more than she claimed. He was probably trying to gauge whether or not Lainey Jo was going to implicate him alongside Uncle Chris.

Oh, Dad.

Once the thumb drive got into the appropriate hands—not Uncle Chris's—her father's worst concern would come true. Lainey Jo would be pivotal in bringing justice to his front door.

But wasn't that what she had to do? She had no choice. People's lives were being violated and ruined all for the sake of the Ludlow name and bank account. Drugs, trafficking, it was a foundation made of sand, and Dad had to know that. It couldn't last forever. He was clinging to it with all of his might, and now, it had blinded him not only against his brother, but against his innocent daughter.

She couldn't even think about her mother. How it would affect her! And thank the Lord, Lainey Jo was an only child and didn't need to consider siblings caught in the crosshairs!

An owl warbled in the woods not far from Lainey Jo, jerking her attention back to the present moment. A cool breeze riffled through her shirt, chilling her arms and causing goose bumps to rise on her skin. Lainey Jo could hear the creek in the distance, even if she couldn't see it. She strained to listen for the sound of Uncle Chris stalking through the woods, but all was silent.

It was the illusion of a peaceful night.

A calm in a storm that she had a feeling was still about to get much worse.

Dozing off had not been part of her plan. In fact, it had been downright foolhardy. Lainey Jo woke with a start, having slid down onto the earth, using the forest floor for a pillow. Now, eyes wide, she strained to see through the darkness. With no idea of the time, Lainey Jo shifted her gaze upward through the treetops, trying to assess with her limited skills if the sky would give her any inclination as to how many hours of darkness she had before daylight.

A few stars peeked out. The cloud covering had thinned, and the moon was able to illuminate the earth with a deep blue glow. Lainey Jo returned her attention to her surroundings. Regardless of the moon, the forest remained dark. But now, the owl had fallen silent. Birds were still. There were no crickets. No nighttime scuffling of a mouse in the grass. The breeze had gone to sleep and taken with it all the natural sounds of the night.

She could hear if Uncle Chris was in the woods, but there was no sound of him either. Had she truly succeeded in evading him? Or had he given up, returned to his truck, and left her alone in the wilderness?

Lainey Jo couldn't imagine the latter was true. He still needed the thumb drive. There was no way he was going to give up that easily. So then, where was he? The fact that he'd not come upon her caused Lainey Jo to debate whether it was safer to stay put than to continue with her plan to find the truck and hopefully escape in it.

Would Bowen come? How could he? He'd have no idea where she was. Not to mention, he was still more in the dark than she was as to who had been shooting at them. He didn't know Uncle Chris was free and trying to divert them with his bullets and, in a twisted way, keep them alive. He also didn't know that the man in black was a hired hit man who'd killed Marshal Halloway and was intent on doing the same to her and Uncle Chris.

No. She was alone for the moment, and she had to consider that was her fate. She had to figure this out on her own. Like anyone in her shoes. Most desperate people didn't have navy SEALs in their back pockets. They had their intuition, their skills—whatever they may include—and their sheer determination.

Lainey Jo stood up, staying close to the aspen that had been her safe place for the last period of time. She had something else too. She had faith. Faith that God would get her home—to Bowen and Gramma Lou and Pax.

She frowned. That was strange. To even think of those people as home. They were strangers mere days ago, but now, they felt like family. Maybe it was trauma that had pushed them together, but Lainey Jo couldn't believe it was only that.

God had pushed them together.

She wasn't sure how it benefited Bowen and the others, but up until this point, Lainey Jo knew how it had benefited her.

"Thank You." Her whispered gratitude was all the noise she was willing to make right now.

Lainey Jo drew in a steadying breath. Okay. She could do this. She would head toward the creek now, cross it, and then wind her way to the truck. It couldn't take more than an hour. At least she didn't think it could. And with another glance up at the sky, Lainey Jo had a feeling dawn was going to begin breaking right about the time she made it to the truck. Whether that was good or not, she had no idea.

Maybe Uncle Chris had read her mind and was waiting there for her. Then what would her next move be?

She had to get going. Staying here was not an option.

Lainey Jo picked her way through the darkness, careful not to get hung up on hidden branches and unseen obstacles. It was impossible to move quickly, but she was less worried about speed than stealth.

She'd managed to go a few hundred yards when she heard a branch snap. Lainey Jo stilled. She strained to listen as her heart rate increased. Probably a deer, or some sort of wildlife, hidden from her vision due to the night.

Lainey Jo started forward again, more anxious now to move fast. She caught her toe on a rock, but caught herself by stabilizing her hand against a tree.

Rustling from deep in the woods alerted her again. Lainey Jo stalled, willing it to be an animal that would show itself to be harmless. She narrowed her eyes, wishing she had some of Bowen's night vision gear. If it were Uncle Chris, he'd be at the same disadvantage as she was. They would both be listening for the other in order to gain an idea of their positions.

A few more breathless moments passed without further sound. Lainey Jo drew in a steadying breath and made a move to start forward again.

But this time, it was unmistakable. A crack of someone stepping on a fallen branch echoed through the silence. And then, more terrifying than the sound of Uncle Chris's voice, was the unfamiliar, throaty laughter of someone she could only assume was the man in black.

He had found her.

Just as Uncle Chris had said he would.

THIRTEEN

Dawn was creeping over the horizon, but it was quickly shut out as the trees closed in on Pax's truck. They had turned onto the barely used road that Pax had referred to on the GPS. Now, he pulled over and into an area of thick shrubs, not seeming to worry about the way they scratched the sides of his vehicle.

He put the truck into Park. "We'll stop here. Any closer and we run the risk of alerting the assailants."

Bowen was ready. He shoved open the door without a word, hopping out onto the ground. Small flashlight in hand, he walked to the wannabe road, which was, in reality, a trail that carved its way through grass and shrubbery, with deep potholes that would make an average vehicle bottom out.

"If the shooter took Lainey Jo here, he had to have a truck," Pax observed. "Even then, a guy could rip up a good undercarriage."

"No joke." Bowen squatted by one of the deeper potholes that was the length of about two tires and the same width. Water pooled in the bottom of it, which was a blessing. He swept the soft light toward the end of the pothole. There was evidence of fresh tire tracks marking the mud. "Someone's been through here."

"Yeah. There are tracks here, too," Pax agreed from his position further down. "We're on the right trail." Satisfaction tinged his words.

Bowen wasn't as optimistic. "Or we're tracking elk hunters."

Pax didn't reply, which was a sure sign he agreed, but didn't like Bowen's conclusion.

They veered into the wooded area off the road. Avoiding being seen was pivotal. He didn't have navy-issued gear, but Bowen was grateful he'd made sure he still had equipment he was accustomed to. He adjusted his night-vision goggles, peering into the range ahead of him. The green glow made shadows come alive. Pax was to his right, giving him a hand signal to go ahead. Bowen gripped his rifle, pointing the barrel toward the ground, and carefully picked his way through the underbrush. There was no sign of human life anywhere, but there was something in his gut that told him they were on the right course.

It had been a long time since he'd gone on faith without sight of any kind. There was no one in his ear calling out coordinates or orders. There was no proof positive that Lainey Jo was even out here. There was no identity as to who they were ultimately up against, nor even what they may be walking into.

It was all faith. And definitely not faith in himself. He'd lost that ages ago.

A low whistle alerted him, and Bowen directed his sight to Pax. His teammate's hand signals indicated he'd spotted something. He motioned for Bowen to go to the left, and without question, Bowen did. They put distance between them, but both maneuvered toward an opening in the forest, where the road connected to a pull-out.

Bowen wanted to shout. There it was. A pickup truck. It wasn't outfitted for hunting, so he could only pray it belonged to the shooter. He caught Pax's attention. Pax waved Bowen toward the truck with the signal that he would cover him.

Satisfied Pax had his six, Bowen snuck into the clearing and up to the truck. It was empty. There was no sign of anyone, including Lainey Jo. He tried the door on the driver's side, and it opened without resistance. The vehicle had little inside of it. A paper map was on the passenger seat. A used coffee thermos in the cupholder. It was an extended cab, so Bowen popped open the half door to the narrow back seat.

Bingo.

A rifle lay on the seat. It was a .308 and equipped with a scope. It had to be the sniper's rifle. A duffel was unzipped on the floor of the truck behind the driver's seat. Bowen checked it. Ammunition and a few other items occupied it.

He frowned, reaching for a black notebook. When he opened it, a bent photograph fell from its pages. Bowen retrieved it and unfolded it.

Lainey Jo's face stared back at him. She was younger in the photo, and his night vision didn't do her features justice. A smile was on her face. She looked carefree. It was a version of Lainey Jo he'd never seen before. For a brief second, he wondered what it would be like to spend a day with Lainey Jo where they hadn't a care in the world and there was no fear of a sniper's rifle being trained on them at any moment.

Bowen replaced the photo in the notebook where he'd found it. He rifled through the pages and saw notes logging

Lainey Jo's routine. There was a phone number scribbled on one page. On the next was a crude sketch of a man in a stocking cap. There was an X across his face. Was the sniper after the other shooter?

Unsure how to interpret that, or if he was even right in his assumption as to who the sketch was of, Bowen thumbed through the rest of the pages, finding most of them blank. He shoved the notebook back into the duffel bag and shut the doors on the truck. Making his way back to Pax, and with dawn lighting the sky, Bowen tipped his night goggles up from where they attached to his hat. He could see enough now to have his footing and catch sight of anyone lurking.

Pax was positioned at the edge of the clearing. When Bowen approached without subtlety, Pax stood.

"What'd you find?" he asked.

"You were right." And Bowen was thankful for Pax's intuition. "It's the sniper's truck. His gun is in the back."

"He left his rifle?" Pax drew his brows together in disbelief.

"Yeah." Bowen nodded in agreement. That it was out of character for any gunman was obvious. "There was a photograph of Lainey Jo. And, he'd sketched out a guy that seems to fit the description of the other shooter."

Pax frowned. "He drew a picture of his partner?"

"That's just it," Bowen replied. "I'm not sure they're partners. He had an X over the guy's face."

Pax adjusted his stance, keeping his rifle pointed down. "Are you saying the sniper is hunting the other shooter?"

"And Lainey Jo?" Bowen nodded. "Yeah, I think I am."

"What kind of mess has your woman gotten herself into?"

"She's not my woman."

"Sure. Keep telling yourself that." Pax rubbed his hand over his eyes and let out a deep breath. "All right. What's our next move?"

Bowen debated their options. Lainey Jo could have been marched off into the woods to be gotten rid of. His gut clenched at the idea. But then, he'd have to assume the sniper had a handgun or was alternatively armed. And why go off into the woods when they were already deep into Timbuktu?

The other idea was—and he liked this one better—Lainey Jo had made a run for it. It made sense then that the shooter had left his gear behind. It was sudden and un-expected. But that meant Lainey Jo was out there some-where, still running, being hunted.

He shared his theories with Pax, who nodded as he lis-tened.

"I'd guess Lainey Jo made a run for it," Bowen con-cluded.

"Atta girl," Pax muttered.

"So we need to track her."

Pax considered. "And what about the other shooter?"

Bowen scowled. "We haven't seen any sign of him."

"If we found your sniper," Pax reasoned, "we have to assume he did also."

"Right."

"I agree we need to go after Lainey Jo, but we have to keep our guard up," Pax said. "We can't assume we're only dealing with one hostile."

Bowen swallowed bile as it rose in his throat. The idea of Lainey Jo out there while two more experienced men chased her through rough territory?

"They better watch it when I find them," Bowen gritted through his teeth.

"You and me both, *compadre*." Pax echoed the sentiment. "You and me both."

She ran. She had no choice. Lainey Jo catapulted through the trees, pushing branches out of her way and ducking under lower limbs of the aspen and pine. She heard him crashing behind her, and all Lainey Jo could do as she ran was repeat, "Please God, please God." She didn't even know what she was asking for beyond some sort of intervention. In her gut, Lainey Jo knew this was going to become a showdown between her and the man in black once again. She didn't think she could best him like she had in the alley. He'd be guarded against her going for his eyes or his groin. He knew she'd fight, and she knew he'd be ready.

The sound of the creek grew as Lainey Jo flew toward it. She scurried down an embankment, dropping to her backside and sliding down it rather than trusting her feet not to trip and sending her rolling. At the bottom, Lainey Jo leapt up, making her way to the creek.

She shot a look over her shoulder.

He was at the top of the embankment.

Lainey Jo knew she could gain more distance if she could traverse the creek fast enough. But creeks in Wyoming weren't like creeks she'd grown up near out East. These creeks were wide, maybe not deep, but the water moved swiftly. Having crossed it once already, Lainey Jo knew the bottom to be made of uneven stones that were both slippery and unstable.

She held out her arms for balance as she plowed into the water. Cold wetness soaked through her canvas tennis shoes, biting at her toes. A stone rolled beneath her right foot, and Lainey Jo yelped as she wobbled wildly in an attempt not to go in.

He was still coming. She could hear the man in black expertly running down the embankment that had threatened to trip her up. If he were that adept, the creek would be less of an issue for him than she'd hoped.

Lainey Jo whimpered as her foot slipped again and her knee came down on a rock. Water saturated her jeans. The collision of rock to knee stung, but she'd been able to soften the blow by catching herself on another boulder sticking up out of the water. Lainey Jo held on to it as she regained her footing, and then, blessedly, she made it to the other side.

Once on solid ground, she ignored the slosh of her shoes as she propelled herself forward. Her only hope now was to somehow get to Uncle Chris's truck before the man caught up to her. That would be a feat in itself, and that would be assuming Uncle Chris's truck was even still there. Lainey Jo had no idea where he was now.

The sudden thought sliced through her mind.

What if the man in black had killed him?

Maybe that was why Uncle Chris had disappeared, giving Lainey Jo the illusion that she could rest. That she was no longer being chased.

It was a terrifying thought, but Lainey Jo knew, not unrealistic.

She hurdled a downed tree and, in another time and place, would have been proud of her track prowess— something she'd never had before. Maybe adrenaline and necessity brought out the hidden talents. But for now, she didn't care.

Lainey Jo couldn't hear the man in black anymore. All she could hear was her heavy breathing, and the worst of it was the painful stitch in her side. She was running out of energy, out of ability, and she had yet to make the small clearing and the truck.

Was this what it was like to live one's last moments? To be chased by death itself and know, deep down inside, that everything you'd done up until now to avoid it was for nothing?

It was futile. Lainey Jo knew that now. Even if she made it to the truck, then what? Would Uncle Chris be there to take out her father's hit man? Eventually, he'd turn on her whether or not he'd promised not to. He wanted the drive, and she wasn't going to give it to him. She didn't even *have* it to give to him. But more than likely, if the truck was there, Uncle Chris wouldn't be, and the odds weren't great that he'd have conveniently left the keys dangling in the ignition.

So then, what would she do? Climb into the cab and lock the doors until the man in black shot out the windows to get to her?

There was no way Lainey Jo would be able to run hard enough or fast enough to put distance between her and him. There was no way to hide.

It was over.

Lainey Jo knew it.

It slowed her steps as defeat whirled in her mind. As branches slapped her face. As long grass tangled around her feet.

It was all coming to an end. Right here. Right now.

Arms wrapped around her legs, and Lainey Jo was thrown to the ground. She kicked out, her foot connecting with some part of her assailant. He grunted, and there was a moment he released her. Lainey Jo scraped at the ground with her hands. Clawing the dirt to pull herself away from her attacker. She managed to get to her knees, but a hand snaked around her ankle.

Kicking wildly, Lainey Jo's efforts paid off. As she sensed her temporary freedom, she lurched to her feet and sprinted forward.

The clearing!

She could see it through the trees. She caught sight of the green polish of Uncle Chris's truck. A spark of hope gave Lainey Jo the energy to push herself forward.

Twenty yards.

Fifteen yards.

He was behind her. Closing the gap.

Ten yards.

Lainey Jo could feel his fingers brush her shirt. She twisted away and burst into the clearing, but she wasn't fast enough. Her assailant launched into her, slamming her against the side of the truck with a crash.

She screamed, striking out with her fists.

"Give me the drive!" Her attacker manhandled her into a semblance of submission, pressing his body full-length against hers.

Lainey Jo was sandwiched between him and the truck. She could see into his eyes. There was no soul in them. She was a job to be completed, and that was all. To him, she was not even a person.

"I don't have it!" Lainey Jo wrestled to free herself.

He took her by her wrists and slammed her hands against the truck's window. Her knuckles bounced off the glass. He wedged his leg between hers, rendering her unable to kick out.

She was pinned.

"Give me the drive, and I'll let you go."

"No, you won't," she argued. "I know my father hired

you. I know he wants you to keep me out of his way." Lainey Jo watched the man's expression. A small part of her still held hope that Uncle Chris had told an elaborate story and that her father wasn't behind this.

But the man's reaction was all too confirming. "Tell me where the drive is and I'll let you down easy."

"Or what?" Lainey Jo spat back.

He leaned in close, and she turned her head away. She could almost feel violence oozing from him.

"Or I'll *make* you tell me where it is."

"And then you'll kill me?" She challenged him.

"And then I'll do what I was hired to do."

Lainey Jo turned her face back toward his. She tried not to flinch as his eyes gored into hers. Evil. Pure evil. "If I knew, I would tell you."

"Did your uncle get it already?" The man's eyes darkened.

Lainey Jo digested the question. If he had to ask that, then it was probable Uncle Chris was still alive.

"How much is my father paying you?" she asked.

"You want to know how much your life is worth?" he taunted in return.

"No," Lainey Jo admitted. "I already know it's worth nothing to him."

The piercing sound of a gunshot shattered the air. A bullet slammed into the man in black's shoulder.

With a shout, he spun Lainey Jo around and in front of him. She was a human shield now, held against him by his arm around her neck. The cold, awful feeling of the barrel of a gun being held to her temple stilled her instantly.

He'd pulled a gun. He was holding her hostage now, and whoever had shot at him had a choice to make.

She prayed that by some chance, it was Bowen in the

woods. That he had been the one to shoot, and that now, he would take the man out, and she could drop to the ground and safety.

But in her spirit, Lainey Jo knew it was Uncle Chris. And if she was right, then either way, the outcome of today was not going to be good.

Thumb drive in hand or not.

FOURTEEN

Bowen and Pax maintained their positions. Unmoving and silent. Bowen crouched behind a tree, shielded by shrubbery, his rifle trained on the man who now held Lainey Jo. Pax lay on his stomach yards to Bowen's right, his own rifle ready to do its thing at the pull of a trigger.

But neither of them had shot their rifles so far. Not yet. And still, there was a bullet hole in Lainey Jo's assailant's shoulder.

They exchanged glances. Bowen knew what Pax was thinking.

Who had taken a shot?

It had all happened so fast. They'd been planning their strategy to go after Lainey Jo when she had burst into the clearing, the man in black on her heels. They'd immediately taken up their positions, but with the attacker in front of Lainey Jo, neither had a clear shot without the threat of their bullet traveling through their mark and into the woman they were trying to save. Thank God that this unknown shot hadn't had the same outcome.

"I want the drive!" the man holding Lainey Jo prisoner shouted.

All was silent.

The man shouted again. "Give me the drive, and I'll give you the girl!"

Pax and Bowen frowned at each other. They remained silent, not revealing their positions.

Now the man was getting agitated. He spun toward the direction the bullet had come from. It was east of Pax. Lainey Jo dragged her feet, making it more difficult for the man to maneuver, but he managed to keep her in front of him in spite of the fact blood soaked his shirt. He seemed unfazed by pain.

"You know I'll kill her!" He tried again. "It's what I was paid to do." There was coldness in the hit man's voice. A frightening disconnect from humanity.

Bowen raised his gun. A few more steps and he'd have a clear angle to the man's head. He could take him out.

Pax's hand signals confirmed he was on the same page.

"I'll come after you." The man was still shouting.

Lainey Jo was smart enough to hang her weight on the man's arm, digging her chin into his forearm.

Good job, Tadpole.

Bowen hoped she'd somehow hear the subliminal encouragement. It was smart to make it more difficult for her assailant to use her as a human shield. By burrowing her chin into his skin, it would bruise him, and it would make her dead weight.

Just another foot.

Bowen's finger hovered over the trigger.

"Maybe we can make a deal!" The hit man tried again. This time he took a step forward.

Bowen winced. That was a worse angle. He shot a look at Pax. Pax shook his head.

No go.

"Pay me for the girl and I won't kill her. Pay me enough

and I'll disappear. You can keep the hard drive, you can keep the girl. I'm good with that."

The idea that the man was so cavalier about bargaining over Lainey Jo's life incensed Bowen. The hardest thing to do was to remain patient. To remain still. Everything in him wanted to leap out and fire a kill shot. But if he missed, if the man moved suddenly, it could take out Lainey Jo.

That was a risk Bowen was not willing to take.

"What? No deal?" The hit man laughed.

A gunshot split the air.

Lainey Jo's scream knifed through Bowen as she crumpled to the ground.

The hit man fell dead in a pool of blood.

Pax jerked his hand to the right.

Bowen nodded.

The shot had come from the same direction as the first one. Only this time, the bullet made its mark. Whoever wielded the gun was a sure shot. Bowen knew the .308 was still in the back of the sniper's truck, and the sound of the *crack-pop* told Bowen it was likely a 9mm handgun that had taken the shot. The shooter may not be an accurate sniper, but he was spot on with his pistol. Which made him even more deadly.

Lainey Jo lay crumpled on the ground, but Bowen could see her beginning to move.

He thanked God she appeared to be all right. It took every ounce of self-restraint not to rush out to her. But the threat hadn't been neutralized yet, and she was still in the middle of danger.

Movement from the east snagged Bowen's attention.

A man exited the tree line, gripping his pistol with both hands, but pointing it away from Lainey Jo.

Bowen readied to take the shot. One bullet and it would be over. He got his nod from Pax.

"What did you do?" Lainey Jo's cry made Bowen freeze.

She pushed away from the dead man on the ground, clambering to her feet. Her shirt was covered in blood spatter. Specks of blood dotted her face and neck. She stared incredulously at the man in black.

"I killed him." The shooter drew close to her, and Bowen continued to hold.

If Lainey Jo knew him—if he was on the right side of things—there was no way Bowen should take the shot.

"Did you want me to let him live? He was going to kill you, Lainey Jo!"

Lainey Jo stepped back from the man advancing on her. Her body language screamed distrust of him. Bowen could see she was trembling. Her knees were weak, and she hung onto the side mirror of the truck for support.

"You killed him," she repeated.

She was going into shock.

Concern flooded Bowen, and by the expression on Pax's face yards away, he knew he wasn't the only one who'd noticed. He kept his gun trained on the man.

He needed more before he could be confident in taking him out. He needed more!

Bowen fought the sense of urgency rising in him. It was a situation not unlike this that had put the American woman into the direct line of fire. It was Bowen's miscalculation as he took the shot along with the sudden and unexpected explosion of an IED in the same moment, that made the entire mission go sideways.

Pax was thrown into the air.

Bowen's bullet drove into the side of the building.

The hostile dropped the American woman with his gun and then aimed at Bowen, who had taken hard impact from the IED. A teammate dropped the hostile with a shot.

The trajectory of life itself had shifted in a split second.

The woman was dead.

Pax was in bad shape, and Bowen could only lie there, unable to move.

Their careers as active duty SEALs were over.

That they were both alive and both able to do what they were doing now was a gift. But the instant flashback caused Bowen's eyes to blur.

He shook his head to clear his vision.

Black shutters began to close in the corners of his eyes. *Dear God, please help.*

He couldn't have it happen again. He couldn't watch Lainey Jo fall from a bullet that he should have stopped. He jerked the butt of the rifle tight against his shoulder. He could see Pax from the corner of his eye, in his position on the ground, giving him the signal to hold.

Hold.

Hold.

If he held, Lainey Jo would be dead.

If he didn't hold, he might shoot an innocent man.

Bowen's hands began to shake.

His heart rate had risen to a rhythmic pounding.

He could take the guy out. Just one shot. And if there were more somewhere in the woods, he could open fire. He could—

Bowen wrestled with his irrational thoughts.

Panic was setting in. It happened. He was human. But he was trained to withstand.

Control yourself.

He inhaled, counting to four. Holding his breath, he counted to four again.

He didn't have time for this!

Bowen made himself exhale on another four-count.

Hold.

One, two, three, four.

And again.

He sensed movement by his feet.

Pax.

His teammate had crawled on his stomach to Bowen's side.

"Slow is smooth, smooth is fast." Pax's whisper penetrated Bowen's fog.

He looked down at Pax.

"Control your breathing." Pax flashed four fingers, four times.

Bowen followed instructions.

"We have to hold. We don't know who this guy is." Pax fell back into hand signals to avoid any further potential disturbance.

Hold.

Breathe.

Slow is smooth, smooth is fast.

Balance.

Precision.

The shutters on his eyes dissipated.

Bowen's hands steadied.

Lainey Jo needed him. She was the task at hand. His next right action was to train his gun on the target and hold.

He could do it.

Bowen added one more step. He breathed a prayer.

Failure was not an option.

* * *

"You killed him." Lainey Jo stared at Uncle Chris.

He held his gun with both hands. She could tell he was ready to lift and fire it again if need be. But at who? At her?

Her legs and body were trembling, so much so that she grappled to hold on to the truck's side mirror. In doing so, her foot accidentally kicked the dead man.

She looked down at him. The man in black was no longer a threat. But now what? Uncle Chris wanted the drive, and she didn't have it.

"I would've killed him earlier if he hadn't gotten away from me when I found you in the woods. Are you all right?" Uncle Chris asked, but he remained stiff and at the ready. There was a wild look in his eyes that made alarms go off within Lainey Jo. "Are you all right?" he repeated.

"I—I'm fine."

No, she wasn't. She wasn't even slightly fine. How was this all to end?

Uncle Chris released his left hand from his gun and held it palm forward, a sign that he didn't intend to hurt her. He took a step toward Lainey Jo.

She clutched the side mirror tighter.

"Listen to me, Lainey Jo. We can do this together. Okay? You and me. We'll go get the drive. We can use it against your father, and we'll be fine. I promise."

Was he asking her to be part of the disgusting nature of the Ludlow "family business"?

Lainey Jo shook her head vehemently. "No. I won't."

"Think about it." Uncle Chris took another step toward her. There was a plea in his voice, and for a moment, Lainey Jo did think about it. "With your dad out of the way, we can rebuild. *You* can rebuild. Everything the family established doesn't have to be lost. You're innocent in all of this.

They'll never charge you with anything. You're the next in line to take over! With Scott in prison, and my conviction being up for a retrial, we can make this happen!"

Lainey Jo blinked, trying to clear her vision. What he said made sense. Didn't it? Could she right the wrongs of her father? And if Uncle Chris could be redeemed, she would have part of her family back.

Hope sparked across her uncle's face. He took another cautious step toward her, his hand still extended. It was like she was the one holding the gun, and he was trying to talk her down. But instead, Uncle Chris had the weapon and *believed* she held the key. The drive. The drive whose whereabouts, she, at this moment didn't know. She had no idea where it had gone when Pax had left the cabin with it and Gramma Lou.

"We can make this happen, Lainey Jo," Uncle Chris repeated.

"But Dad—"

"He deserves prison time. The rest of his life."

Yes. Uncle Chris was right.

"And you can help put him there. It'll be the first big step in righting the wrongs."

Lainey Jo nodded. Yes. She had already done it once with Uncle Chris, and—she met her uncle's eyes and frowned.

No. She *had* done it once with Uncle Chris, who deserved the same consequences as her father did. There was no justice for their victims if she followed her uncle's line of thinking. She would be manipulated and used, and Lainey Jo knew without a doubt that Uncle Chris had no intention of ending the darkness that their family had orchestrated. He only planned to use her as a pawn to overtake her father's control and make himself the head of it all.

"No." She shook her head, reason returning. She might die here. She might die at the hands of her uncle, but Lainey Jo knew she would never work alongside him ever again.

"No?" Uncle Chris stiffened.

"I won't do it."

"Then give me the drive, Lainey Jo." Uncle Chris lifted his gun, his left hand coming up to encircle the grip.

"No." Lainey Jo clung to the side mirror.

"Give me the drive." Uncle Chris's voice turned to steel.

"I won't." She shook her head.

"Give me the drive!" he yelled, shaking the gun at her. Lainey Jo cried out.

Her uncle cleared the distance between them, the gun inches from her forehead. There was no more mercy on his face, no more empathy in his eyes. This. This was the uncle she had helped condemn in court. This was the man who was, for all intents and purposes, identical to the brother he wished to take down.

"I won't do it. I don't have it," Lainey Jo sobbed.

"I want the drive!" Uncle Chris pressed the gun to her head.

"Just shoot me!" Lainey Jo screamed. "Get it over with and shoot me!"

"Stop!"

Lainey Jo and Uncle Chris froze.

Bowen stepped from the woods. His rifle was in his right hand, but he was lowering it to the ground as he held up his left hand. "Don't do anything stupid, Chris." He addressed Lainey Jo's uncle. His eyes shifted to hers.

She couldn't read what he was trying to communicate, but in her mind, she could hear what he'd told her in the past.

Stay put.

Uncle Chris's hand shook, the gun playing an ominous tap dance against her forehead.

Bowen took another careful step toward them. "I have the drive."

Uncle Chris jerked his head toward Bowen.

Bowen nodded. "I know where it is. I can get it for you."

"Where is it?" Uncle Chris didn't lower the gun.

"I have it in a safe place," Bowen answered.

Uncle Chris laughed. "Sure you do!"

"I do! It's back at the cabin. It's back in the stuffed cat, and the cat is on the table."

Lainey Jo knew that wasn't true.

Bowen's eyes sparked a warning.

Stay put.

"Then go get it. Bring it back here." Uncle Chris held his stance.

"Uh-uh. No. That's not how it's going to work." Bowen shook his head.

Another step.

Stay put.

"Then tell me how it's going to work!" Uncle Chris seethed.

"You're going to put the gun down."

"Not a chance!"

"You're going to put the gun down," Bowen tried again. "Then you and I will take the truck and go back to the cabin. You can have the drive. You can leave Lainey Jo here where she's safe. Once you have the drive, we'll part ways. Lainey Jo's mine. The drive is yours."

"How do I know you'll keep your word?"

The gun tapped against her forehead.

Lainey Jo whimpered.

She kept her eyes trained on Bowen. He gave a slight shake of his head. His lips moved ever-so-slightly.

Stay put.

"You don't." Bowen was closing the gap between them now. A few more steps, and Lainey Jo knew he could leap forward and take out Uncle Chris. But if he did that, the gun might go off. She'd be dead in an instant.

"You've got to trust me," Bowen stated for Uncle Chris, but his eyes were fixed on Lainey Jo's.

She gave a slight nod.

"I don't trust anyone," Uncle Chris snarled. "Least of all, you." He swung the gun away from Lainey Jo toward Bowen.

"Stay low!" Bowen's shout echoed in the air.

Lainey Jo dropped to the ground.

A gunshot penetrated the air.

Uncle Chris dropped.

Lainey Jo hustled away from him.

Away from Bowen.

She saw Pax emerge from the woods. He had taken the shot. Bowen had been the distraction. She had followed orders.

Uncle Chris was dead.

She could see him. Lying there next to the hit man.

"Target neutralized." Pax's words were low and meant for Bowen's ears.

But Lainey Jo heard them. Uncontrollable shakes took over her body. She pushed herself further away from them, uncaring that the earth dug into her legs and backside. Her fingers clawed in the dirt as she moved backward.

Bowen crouched low, stretching out his hand. "It's over."

She could see the icy blue of his eyes. Strong. Sure. Confident.

Mission success.

But her? What about her?

She continued to shake, staring at Bowen as if he might charge at her. She was cornered. Cornered by life. It had her by the throat. All of it. Her father had taken a hit out on her. Her uncle had tried to kill her. And now? She was here. On the ground of the Bighorn Mountains, in an unfamiliar area, surrounded by pines and aspen and natural beauty and everything good marred by everything destructive and horrible.

"Lainey Jo." Bowen's voice tried to break through the muddle of her mind.

She shook her head. Her breaths were coming fast, her body threatening to pass out.

"Lainey Jo." His voice again.

Safe. He was safe.

Lainey Jo could see herself in her mind's eye. She saw herself leaping into his truck for the first time. She saw him driving her to Gramma Lou's. She saw him reach out and hold her.

She met his eyes. This time, instead of strength and confidence, she saw concern and a deep well of sacrificial care for her. When had she ever seen that in the eyes of a man who was supposed to care for her? A selfless service? A willingness to put her life, her value, before his own?

"Look at me." It was a gentle command. The kind she knew was intended to ground her. To calm her.

So she did. She locked eyes with Bowen. He drew closer, crouching next to her. He was a soldier. He was a warrior. He was anything but a failure.

"Mission success," she whispered.

There was a flicker in his eyes and then his soft echo. "Yeah. Mission success."

FIFTEEN

She hadn't asked what had happened after Bowen and Pax had extracted her from the wilderness site where the bodies of the hit man and Uncle Chris lay. She just knew that it was mere hours before the FBI and the US Marshals were next to her in the hospital. There were questions. So many questions that the doctor ordered them to stay out. Lainey Jo didn't think the FBI really appreciated that, but when the doctor came back in, he stood over Lainey Jo's bed and issued her a reassuring smile.

"You have a mild concussion. Considering what you've been through, you're in remarkably good shape. But they don't need to know that."

It had been three days since the event had taken place.

Now, she sat in a meeting room at the local police station. An agent in a suit with a tie that was a swath of grays and blues sat opposite her. Another agent stood off to the side.

Here came the questions.

She knew it was going to come, but she wasn't sure she was ready for it. How did a daughter prepare to give testimony against her own father? Sure, Bowen had tried to give her the factual argument that it was her father's consequences, not hers, but it didn't make the pill any easier to swallow.

"We have the drive your uncle made," the agent started. "We wanted to tell you that as of this morning, your father has been taken into custody."

"And my mother?" Lainey Jo didn't even know what to do about her mother. Their relationship had always been a distant one.

"She'll remain at their home. For now."

"What do I do now?" Lainey Jo asked.

"Well," the agent leaned back in his chair. "You've been through this before. It's a long process. In the meantime, we'll put you in protective custody. When it's over, you'll have the option to relocate in the Witness Protection Program. A new name, new identity, new—"

"New place to live," Lainey Jo finished. There was no relief in the victory of escaping Uncle Chris. She had traded one woe for another. Her father. And, where Uncle Chris had been a potential threat for vengeance, Dad had already put a hit out on her. It was inevitable he would try from prison.

"It's not ideal," the agent admitted.

"No." Lainey Jo raised her eyes. "It's not."

An image of Gramma Lou flashed through her mind. She had been foolish to harbor even the tiniest of hopes that she could return to Gramma Lou's cabin in the Bighorns, sit on the front porch swing with a cup of coffee, and find respite. And Bowen? Who even was he to her now? A hero, yes, but a friend? More? Less? He had checked in on her every day since the incident. The man had practically slept outside of her hospital door. If the FBI hadn't sent him away with their own security, she had a feeling Bowen would be next to her right now. Gauging everything they said. Cataloging it in his mind. Planning options for the next course of action.

But there was no other course of action.

It was WITSEC. It would always be WITSEC.

Lainey Jo sagged back in her chair. She thought of her stale apartment that had been trashed when the man her father had hired tried to find the thumb drive. She'd gone with a Parisian theme. Hailing back to that lonely summer at boarding school. What would she do this next time? Where would she end up? Oregon, maybe. Could she request the East Coast? It was where she was from originally, so probably not. Florida?

"How about Hawaii?" Lainey Jo asked. But there was an edge to her question, and the agents exchanged glances. "Hawaii sounds nice." She tried to swallow back betrayal, anger and loneliness. "It has palm trees and beaches. Don't they grow real pineapples there? Maybe not. I thought they did." She was rambling. "I could sell ice cream on the beach out of a little pink truck." Lainey Jo sucked in a sob.

The agent who was standing took a step forward. He had a gentler face. He was older, gray at his temples. He leaned forward. "I know this is hard—"

"Hard?" Lainey Jo shot back. "You have no idea what hard even is."

It was probably unfair of her, and she was about to apologize when there was a short rap on the meeting room door.

The agent sighed. "I'll check it out." He left Lainey Jo sitting across from the man with the blue-and-gray tie.

He cleared his throat. "Did you want some water?"

"No." She shook her head.

They both heard murmurings outside of the door and then, in a matter of a minute, the agent stepped back into the room. There was a different expression about him. He held his body tighter, and he pressed his lips together as if regretting something.

Tapping the arm of the agent in the chair, he tilted his head and they swapped positions. Lainey Jo was all right with that. She preferred the older agent. He was more fatherly. More like what she wished her father was like.

"I—" he hesitated. "I have some news."

Lainey Jo didn't blink. She stared at him. That familiar sensation of nothing good filled her.

The agent sniffed, folded his hands in front of him, and issued her the most apologetic expression she had ever seen.

"I'm afraid your father is—he's dead."

"What!" Lainey Jo could only stare. Trying to make sense of the words the agent had just spoken.

"They found him in his cell this morning."

"Did he—?" She couldn't finish the sentence.

The agent gave a curt nod. "I'm afraid he wasn't up to the process of an investigation and a trial."

Lainey Jo sagged back in her chair. Tears burned her eyes. She'd not anticipated this. She'd not planned on this. She'd not been prepared for any of it.

"Now what?" she managed.

The agent drew a serious breath and nodded. "Now you can go home."

She stared at him. "That's not my home."

"Where would you like to go, then, Miss Ludlow?"

Lainey Jo started with the use of her real name. Ludlow. She preferred Beckett now. But then the agent's question sank in, and she met his eyes.

"Have you been introduced to Gramma Lou?"

She wanted to go home, and that was the closest to home that Lainey Jo had ever known.

Gramma Lou had gone above and beyond. Her table was full, and the plates around it were already half piled with food. Baked potatoes, green beans, roast beef and home-made dinner rolls.

Years before, Lainey Jo would have considered it traditional American fare and been willing to trade it in for the gourmet meals her wealth had allowed her to make customary. Her favorite had been *Filet de Boeuf Rossini*—a beef tenderloin delectably topped with foie gras, truffle and a Madeira reduction that had made her mouth salivate. But now, as Lainey Jo sat at the rustic table in Gramma Lou's cabin in the middle of the Bighorn Mountains of Wyoming, roast beef looked particularly delicious.

It was made more delightful because of the company around the table. Bowen, who was scarfing down the beef with a rather sad lack of finesse or table manners. His elbows were solidly placed on the tabletop, and he only moved his forearm in order to spear more meat.

Pax sat next to him, cracking silly jokes and remarking that if Gramma Lou had added jalapenos to the beef, he would have said she made better *carne asada* than his own *abuela*. To which Gramma Lou cuffed him gently on the side of the head and reprimanded, "Never tell another woman her cooking is better than your own grandmother's. That's treason."

Laughter had filled the room at that, and Gramma Lou offered more green beans to her pastor and his wife, who rounded out the circle. A "meal of thankfulness," Gramma Lou had said. For all of God's protection and the provision of family to make sure each was safe and cared for.

Lainey Jo observed each person in their seat. The two navy SEALs, a pastor and his wife, whom she had become more acquainted with as the weeks had passed since everything had happened, and Gramma Lou.

"Hold on!" Pax held up his hand, commanding attention. "Everyone, I believe Mr. Rogers here needs the floor."

Bowen lifted his eyes from forking a load of beef toward his mouth.

"I do?" He raised his brows.

"Yeahhhh?" Pax's response was laden with meaning. His dark eyes widened as if Bowen was missing his cue.

"Oh yeah!" Bowen scraped his chair back, and it ground against the wood floor. "I'll be back." He made for the door and exited the cabin.

"That boy." Gramma Lou clicked her tongue.

Within a few seconds, he returned with a small box, a golden bow wrapped around it, and he set it on the table in front of Gramma Lou, pushing back her plate.

"What is this?" She looked between Bowen and Pax.

Lainey Jo was just as curious, and she exchanged an anticipatory smile with the pastor's wife.

"We figured you were owed a little something, Gram," Bowen said. "For all the gunfire you took a while back."

"I think *I* should be the one to repay her," Lainey Jo broke in, a tiny snag of remorse gripping her heart.

Pax wagged his finger at her. "Eh, eh, eh, *chica*. Don't steal the man's thunder."

Gramma Lou untied the ribbon, and it fell to her lap. She lifted the lid, and a little nose peeked out, with white whiskers, followed by a furry black face and white-tipped ears. "A *kitten*?" Gramma Lou pulled back in surprise. She gave Bowen an incredulous look. "Why on earth did you get me a kitten?"

"Because," Bowen dropped a kiss on her gray head, "you said real cats were nice."

"I said they were nicer than stuffed ones!" Gramma Lou

scolded, but her eyes twinkled. "Ohhh, but she is a little darling." The kitten nudged Gramma Lou's hand.

"*He*, Gram," Bowen corrected. "It's a he."

With dinner derailed by the cuteness of the new kitten, Lainey Jo took the chance to slip outside.

The entire evening had been lovely. From a kitten, to supper with a pastor and his wife, to the homemade coziness of a cabin… Truly. It had been lovely.

A tear traced its way down her cheek, and Lainey Jo swiped it away. She couldn't ruin the evening. There was so much to be thankful for.

The front porch boasted a porch swing, and Lainey Jo settled onto it, allowing her gaze to wander. Dusk was settling in, and the hills were taking on a warm golden hue. The lodgepole pines dotted the landscape like guardians, and in the far distance, Lainey Jo could see a bull moose, the silhouette of its flat antlers. It was peaceful here.

The cabin door opened, and Lainey Jo knew without looking that it was Bowen.

"Mind if I sit?" He motioned to the space next to her on the swing.

She didn't answer, but moved over, and Bowen lowered himself, the porch swing swaying with the addition of his weight.

"So," he started.

It was Bowen. He didn't add anything more and didn't take away the word. It was meant to be a conversation starter, but Lainey Jo could tell he had no idea what else to say.

She didn't blame him. What did someone say to someone who just weeks before had their uncle shot in front of them, and then been informed their father had decided to

end things while in prison awaiting trial? Grief was difficult to traverse in the best of relationships. But this?

"I feel guilty," Lainey Jo admitted.

"Guilty?"

"Yes." She nodded, dropping her gaze to her hands and picking at a chipped fingernail. "I'm relieved."

Silence. And then, "Makes sense."

Of course it did. Bowen, ever the realist. The objective one. "You don't have to look over your shoulder anymore."

"I don't have to keep my head on a swivel?" she teased, following it up with a watery laugh.

"That too." He smiled.

"I loved my father. I loved Uncle Chris."

"I know that," Bowen acknowledged.

"But they almost ruined my life," she finished. Her admission caused her to bring her eyes back up to look at Bowen.

He didn't say anything, but she felt his hand move, and then his fingers brushed hers. It was a gesture without pressure, but Lainey Jo didn't hesitate. She moved her hand the rest of the way, and their fingers interlocked.

"A few months ago," Bowen started, "I couldn't see much of a future. I was a failure—at least I thought I was. The fact is, there's nothing anyone can say to make you feel better. I'll always carry some responsibility for the way our last mission went down."

Lainey Jo opened her mouth to protest.

Bowen squeezed her hand to silence her. "But—I also know that I was never in control to begin with. It's okay if I move on with my life."

Lainey Jo was beginning to see what he was trying to say. "It's natural to be relieved while grieving at the same time?"

Bowen nodded. "And while wanting to move on with your life," he finished.

"I wish I knew what that looked like." Lainey Jo regretted her words the instant she'd admitted them. She didn't want to insinuate anything that Bowen might misconstrue.

He chuckled. "You could start with a kitten."

She issued him a surprised look. "Gramma Lou doesn't want that little sweetheart?"

He tipped his head back and forth, wincing a little. "Welllll, she told me she's more of a dog person."

"I'll take it!" Lainey Jo blurted out. "I'll take the kitten."

"She kinda figured you'd say that."

Lainey Jo smiled. A new kitten? A fresh start? Permission to grieve and to experience relief? It was a gift. God had given her a gift in Bowen, and she wasn't sure if Bowen knew it.

"Just don't name the kitten 'Thumbdrive,'" Bowen grimaced.

"Never!" Lainey Jo widened her eyes, and they shared a laugh. "I was thinking…Tadpole."

"Tadpole." Bowen tried the name. "I like it."

"I do too," Lainey Jo concluded.

Bowen tugged on her hand. She turned back to him and their eyes met.

"I like *you*." His voice lowered. A soothing, mesmerizing depth to his words.

Lainey Jo bit her lip nervously.

Bowen's eyes dropped to her mouth, then lifted back to her eyes. "What do you think? You? Me? Tadpole?"

"I think we could give it a try," she breathed.

"You know I've got your six." Bowen leaned in.

"And I've got yours," she whispered.

"Lotta good that'll do," he teased.

She issued his arm a playful slug just as his lips claimed hers. The promise of protection, of loyalty, and many more kisses to come.

* * * * *

If you enjoyed this book, be sure to pick up Jaime Jo Wright's previous Love Inspired Suspense book, Buried Wilderness Secrets. *Available now!*

Dear Reader,

I wanted to share with you where Lainey Jo's name came from. I have a plethora of nieces and nephews. Maybe one day I'll find a way to squeeze all them into a book, but for this book, I chose my niece Lainey. You have to understand, this gal, who will be going on twelve when this book releases, is a tadpole in her own right. And if you don't know what a "tadpole" is in SEAL jargon, it's essentially a SEAL in training.

My niece is tough for being a peanut. She's also the youngest of all my nieces and nephews. And the problem is, when you have so many cousins, a lot of times you get overlooked. She's not. I promise you. But just in case she ever feels like she is, I wanted her to have a name in one of my books. Not to mention, if anyone in my family would have the stamina and guts to become a navy SEAL, it'd be Lainey.

And then there's the "Jo" part of Lainey's name. Now that is *not* because I like my own name. It's because while I was writing this book, my daughter—who at the time was going on sixteen—had refused to read any of the 15+ books I'd written. But while I was writing this book, she decided to pick up my first Love Inspired Suspense and give Mom's writing a whirl. I have the text message to prove it. But the "I love your book!" will live in my heart forever. "Jo" is her middle name, too. She's MY Jo. So Lainey became Lainey Jo. For two very special young women in my life.

You both are going somewhere in life, because God has plans for you. Never underestimate what He will do, and be prepared, you two. It's going to be a wild ride!

Jaime Jo Wright

Get up to 4 Free Books!

We'll send you 2 free books from each series you try
PLUS a free Mystery Gift.

Both the **Love Inspired®** and **Love Inspired® Suspense** series feature compelling novels filled with inspirational romance, faith, forgiveness and hope.

YES! Please send me 2 FREE novels from the Love Inspired or Love Inspired Suspense series and my FREE gift (gift is worth about $10 retail). I may cancel anytime by emailing ReaderServiceInfo@Harlequin.com or by calling 1-800-873-8635. If I don't cancel, I will receive 6 brand-new Love Inspired Larger-Print books or Love Inspired Suspense Larger-Print books every month and be billed just $7.19 each in the U.S. or $7.99 each in Canada. That is a savings of 20% off the cover price. It's quite a bargain! Shipping and handling is just 75¢ per book in the U.S. and $1.75 per book in Canada.* I understand that accepting the free books and gift places me under no obligation to buy anything—they are mine to keep for free no matter what I decide.

Choose one:

- ☐ **Love Inspired Larger-Print** (122/322 BPA G3CD)
- ☐ **Love Inspired Suspense Larger-Print** (107/307 BPA G3CD)
- ☐ **Or Try Both!** (122/322 & 107/307 BPA G3CE)

Name (please print)

Address   Apt. #

City   State/Province   Zip/Postal Code

Email: Please check this box ☐ if you would like to receive newsletters and promotional emails from Harlequin Enterprises ULC and its affiliates. You can unsubscribe anytime.

> Mail to the **Harlequin Reader Service:**
> **IN U.S.A.:** P.O. Box 1341, Buffalo, NY 14240-8531
> **IN CANADA:** P.O. Box 603, Fort Erie, Ontario L2A 5X3

Want to explore our other series or interested in ebooks? Visit www.ReaderService.com or call 1-800-873-8635.

LIRLIS2603